A Pinchbeck Bride

Books by Stephen Anable

The Fisher Boy
A Pinchbeck Bride

A Pinchbeck Bride

A Mark Winslow Mystery

Stephen Anable

Poisoned Pen Press

Poisoned
Pen
Press

Copyright © 2011 by Stephen Anable

First Edition 2011

10 9 8 7 6 5 4 3 2 1

Library of Congress Catalog Card Number: 2010932108

ISBN: 9781590588567 Hardcover
9781590588581 Trade Paperback

Poisoned Pen Press
6962 E. First Ave., Ste. 103
Scottsdale, AZ 85251
www.poisonedpenpress.com
info@poisonedpenpress.com

Printed in the United States of America

To my family

Pinchbeck: An alloy of zinc and copper used as imitation gold.

Chapter One

It had not yet become a "household word," or an attraction as notorious as, say, the site of the Boston Massacre. It had yet to draw the media hordes or their satellite trucks, or to spawn memorial websites with hundreds of flickering virtual candles. No soggy mounds of teddy bears had accumulated on its steps; no bouquets of wilting supermarket flowers spilled from its threshold onto the sidewalk. Mingo House was not yet the site of a nationally famous crime but simply a lesser-known historic property, a four-story brownstone built in 1863 by Corinth Hollis Mingo ("Corinth One"), the armaments manufacturer who had made his fortune during the Civil War.

Mingo House held no artistic masterpieces—no Titians and Roman mosaics like Fenway Court—and no gilded ballrooms like the Newport mansions. Instead, it functioned as a Victorian time capsule because Corinth Mingo's sole surviving child, Corinth Mingo II ("Corinth Two"), had chosen to preserve his childhood in amber, so that future generations could marvel at it—like a prehistoric insect with extravagant wings and obsolete mandibles.

My involvement with Mingo House began with a dream-shattering phone call at eleven-thirty one spring night. I picked up the receiver, dreading some death, some car wreck, to be greeted by the most blasé of voices: "Mark, Mark Winslow? This is Rudy…" He assumed I would know precisely who he was, and, in fact, I'd met no other Rudolph. I recalled meeting

Rudy Schmitz at a fundraiser for the Boston Ballet, when he'd mentioned that his mother, "an incurable romantic," had named him after the Austrian archduke who'd perished with his mistress in the suicide pact at Mayerling.

"Mark, I've just been thinking, you'd make a terrific trustee of Mingo House. What with your advertising savvy and love of history. And your terrific sense of humor, of course."

I think I said Yes just to hang up the phone, just to get back to sleep… How many sleepless nights, how much angst and irritation, that would cost me in the future!

That year, I lived not far from Mingo House, with my partner, Roberto Schreiber, in one of the "luxury" condominiums that went up in Boston during the 1980s. It was a postmodern pile, a federalist brick ziggurat with brass and granite touches, looming above one end of the Public Garden. Ours was one of the smallest units in the complex, but facing the greenery and pond of the park.

Years earlier, Roberto and I had been through hell together, confronting a cult and a kidnapper on Cape Cod. Now, in the new millennium, we were determined to experience crime only through certain select shows on television. Roberto had abandoned his job as a courier—shedding his Spandex and bicycle—to enroll in law school, and I was trimming my standup comedy schedule and considering getting my master's degree in history.

I might have mentioned that to Rudy Schmitz or to one of his friends, because when we spoke later, he quipped, "Perhaps you'll do your thesis on Mingo House. Who knows?" Who indeed?

Before I attended my first meeting of the board of trustees, Genevieve Courson, a young docent, was assigned to "orient" me. This meeting kept being perpetually postponed because… one trustee had a trade show in San Jose, another a big project with the Massachusetts League of Women voters, and Rudy had family business in Baltimore, where his father owned Schmitz Brothers, the city's largest department store.

"Do they ever actually meet?" I asked Genevieve. "The trustees?"

"They have good intentions," she said. "Well, most of them. They're not a tight-knit group, they're all business. They don't socialize outside their involvement with Mingo House."

Genevieve was a junior at Shawmut College and had an internship at Mingo House, working Thursdays and Saturdays. I shadowed her for a number of weeks. She was thin, with the bones of a sparrow and a sharp nose pierced by a ring of all-but-invisible silver. Her short dark hair was singed with henna, and her wide eyes were colored a liquid brown that seemed to drink you in with wonder and curiosity.

On my first day at Mingo House, we had lunch together, just the two of us, at a vegetarian hole-in-the-wall in Copley Square, and decided to take a quick walk in the Back Bay. Genevieve was bundled in a vintage coat of Navy-blue wool over a rayon dress printed with Forties cherry blossoms. On the lapel of her coat she'd fastened a heavy zircon pin in the shape of a comet. She was, she admitted, "a thrift shop junkie." Her favorite, Past Lives, was a couple of blocks away, on Newbury Street.

"How did you hear about Mingo House?" she asked me.

I told her.

"That Rudy's a character," she said.

"How did you? Hear about Mingo House?"

She smiled with both her mouth and her eyes. "My mother brought me. On my tenth birthday, believe it or not. It was my first time at Mingo House and my first ride on the swan boats. It was an ultra-special day."

"So which made the bigger impression?" I was sure it was the swan boats.

"Boy, that's a tight call."

We had come to the entrance to the Public Garden, where the lawns shone with a young green and new leaves were swelling on the weeping willows. In the flowerbeds, pansies trembled in a chill wind and tulips offered the sun their Technicolor cups. The fountains had been partially filled, so that the statues of children—nude, pudgy with pageboy haircuts—played under bright jets of water. The swan boats circled the little pond which was the golden-brown color of root beer.

"Oh, they're back," she said.

The swan boats are narrow, barge-like craft, flat in front with open rows of varnished seats, and ending with a touch of bravado—huge swan-shaped shells containing the college students who paddle them with their feet.

"Oh, let's take a voyage," Genevieve said.

"Are you sure there won't be icebergs?" I teased her.

"The swan boats are unsinkable." She began humming the theme song from *Titanic*, then seized my elbow in her hand and tugged me toward the iron-and-granite bridge spanning the pond; she was strong for such a diminutive person. "Since this is your first day, the voyage is my treat. Welcome to the Mingo family."

Descending the squat steps from the bridge to the swan boats' dock, she took her wallet from her bag, a thrift shop find vivid with gold sequins, and bought us two adult tickets. Our fellow passengers seemed to be all out-of-towners, packing large cameras and small children. The dockside crew requested we shift to the left to balance the boat, and Genevieve giggled. She retained all of the enthusiasm of her ten-year-old self, pointing at the ducks pecking under their wings as they sunned themselves on their green wooden house in the center of the first lagoon. "Oh, aren't they cute? Look at the babies!" We passed under the bridge, into a coolness where chicken wire had been fixed to the bridge girders to discourage pigeons. Genevieve nodded at the cast-iron Japanese lantern on the shore to our left: "That has the most wonderful bas-relief of monkeys. My mother gave me a stuffed monkey that looked just like them." Then we rounded the small island in the second lagoon, which, ringed by boulders and cool with shade, was populated by ducks, sleeping amid the ivy and their discarded down. "I always meant to explore that island. Some winter, when the pond is drained. It's so mysterious." Then she gave me a penetrating stare. "The way inaccessible things always are."

Something about her stare had unnerved me, even though it had lasted only a microsecond. I edged away. "I read that the city spent hundreds of thousands of dollars on that island. Landscaping it with new trees and re-enforcing it. It was eroding, falling apart."

"Like poor Mingo House," Genevieve said.

Then the boat glided flush with the dock, and the crew steadied it as we stepped out.

"I worry about Mingo House, I really do."

That struck me as extraordinary for a person of her age, to feel so keenly about a historic property. "Do you really?"

"Oh, absolutely. It was love at first sight when I saw it. And it really needs help. The brownstone is crumbling like stale fudge, and the roof—why you could take a shower in the library during a good rainstorm. The wallpaper needs conserving, so do most of the paintings." The wind lifted the branches of the willows and the tufts of Genevieve's henna-singed hair.

"Are your parents artists?" I thought that might explain her precocious empathy for old things.

"God, no." She pointed across the pond, toward the base of the Japanese lantern. "Look, the live swans are back. See them together?"

One of the birds submerged its noble head, in quest of an insect or some delicious strand of slime.

"Let's go see them," Genevieve said, and then, abruptly, she wheeled around, changed her mind. "Actually, I'd rather go this way." She commandeered my arm and steered me in the opposite direction, back toward the dock—out of our way, in fact, if we were returning to Mingo House immediately.

When we returned she gave me the tour. "Not the regular tour or the VIP tour. The insiders' tour."

The house was crammed with pretentious walnut and mahogany furniture of the quality to please a nouveau-riche merchant of the mid-nineteenth century. Its walls were sheathed with stout-dark paneling or gilded and embossed wallpapers adorned with berries, vines, and leaves. The rooms were busy with bric-a-brac, with family photographs, and with curtains and upholstery all tassels, embroidery, and fringe. Hung throughout were Italian paintings of classical subjects—the oracle at Delphi, Circe with her pigs, Cleopatra clasping the asp to her neck—done in lustrous, enamel-bright colors. Corinth Hollis Mingo, who had been conceived in Greece, had also purchased plaster casts of the Parthenon frieze, of warriors, slightly yellowed with age, as well as what was possibly the most valuable item on the premises, a painting that some contended was a Millet, of peasants bending in a field of stubble. The Mingoes seemed to be a family of hoarders, throwing nothing away, neither pin cushions nor Worth gowns, curling irons nor salt cellars, so that the diverse stuff of Victorian life, the breadth of the building's contents, made it extraordinary, less museum than time machine.

The Mingoes had arrived in Massachusetts from England in the seventeenth century. "Legend had it" that Barnabas Mingo had played a role in the trial and execution of King Charles I, and had fled with some important ecclesiastical silver, including a royal monstrance. If so, neither he nor his immediate descendants converted this cache into cash. The family subsisted as yeoman farmers for several generations, until Asa Mingo entered the China trade, and his son, Corinth Hollis Mingo, established his armaments factory in Maynard, Massachusetts—just as John Brown was raiding Harpers Ferry.

"Corinth One had timing," Genevieve said.

Genevieve guided me through the building, through Clara's bedroom, Corinth's bedroom, the nursery with its three lemon-wood beds, each holding a fragile stuffed lamb… Our last stop was the library, overlooking Beacon Street. "You could call this the Crisis Room." She described in detail the leaks in its ceiling, which was crumbly, puckered. Then, she blew dust from a copper inkwell featuring a pair of angry eagles. "Would you like to see Clara's private…albums?"

I nodded.

She pulled one of several cardboard Cutty Sark cartons from the bookshelves. Her knees buckled momentarily.

"Do you need help?"

"The weight of history." Genevieve slid the carton onto Corinth One's desk. From it she extracted one of the photographs, which I now saw were ponderous glass plates, about eleven by seventeen inches in size.

I recoiled when I saw what the plate depicted—piles of pale amputated human feet, stacked in the grass outside an army tent.

Then Genevieve produced still more plates, all focused on wounds, corpses, gore—severed arms, suet-white, and two severed human heads, of bearded men, their open eyes startled by death.

The photographs were true portraits of horror, a Victorian Armageddon, Hell under glass. How could Corinth One have tolerated their presence, especially in a house with young children?

"Clara hired Ezra Morton, a rival of Matthew Brady's, to photograph the damage done by Mingo armaments during the Civil War. Both sides used the family's 'products,' so Ezra had plenty of…opportunities."

"Clara did it as a kind of penance. She later became a famous medium, contacting dead soldiers to apologize, and helping their families make contact."

"These…aren't included in your standard tour."

"No. These are for special occasions." I've forgotten: did she smile when she said that?

Chapter Two

Genevieve Courson adored the old place. Ignoring the "Please do not touch" signs, she handled everything: the luminous glass vases, studded with emerald chips and moonstones; the yards of French lace; and the alabaster sphinx on Corinth One's desk, repugnant to me because it had the white translucence of an especially fat grub pulled from the roots of a diseased lawn. She felt compelled to handle them "because you can't get to know things without handling them, can you? The way you can't get to know a city by taking a bus tour. You have to walk and have your feet hit the pavement. You have to have that physical contact."

She would try on the clothing the Mingoes had left hanging in closets or folded with sachets in bureau drawers: a hat crowned with egret plumes, a paisley shawl, a mourning band, a muff of still glossy sable. She seemed determined to leave her DNA on every object in the collection.

She was sensitive, bright, far more intelligent, I thought, than the average Shawmut student. She admitted as much, one day, when we were walking after lunch and she stopped, lingering by the windows of the Ritz Carlton Hotel on Newbury Street. She was admiring the silver. "What an exquisite candelabra!" She could get away with using a pretentious adjective because she was so enthused and not at all facetious. "I have to admit, I like the finer things in life."

"How did you end up a Shawmut?" I said, and her posture collapsed slightly. "Well, I was accepted at Brown and Middlebury, but I needed financial aid and Shawmut was a relative bargain." Then she perked up again: "But I had friends who were going there. That was one good thing. I guess."

She suggested we walk through the Ritz lobby, much more restrained than the Copley Plaza, just marble and brass railings, and low ceilings and stone urns of pale flowers. The bellhops stared at her, not because she was truly beautiful, but because she was striking, a presence. I think the concierge bowed, ever so slightly, as though he knew her.

She wanted to wander through Arlington Street Church, made of the same chocolate-colored sandstone as Mingo House. "Imagine, all of these old buildings rest on wooden piles driven into the mud. Like the buildings in Venice." She inspected the church's Tiffany stained-glass windows. She touched those too, felt the opalescent layers of glass of the saints' robes and the lilies cascading through a window depicting the Madonna. "Tiffany went around his studio with a hammer, and if he found anything he considered substandard, he'd just smash it." I'd heard that story too, but I let her talk, let her have the pleasure of conveying it. "I wonder if Clara Mingo ever came here. This church was built when the Mingoes moved to the Back Bay. And she was spiritual, right?"

I had to be honest. "And slightly mad. To put it charitably."

"Who can say, really? Perhaps she saw another reality. Saw beyond what the average person could comprehend."

"Do you believe in ghosts?"

We were outside the church. A homeless man, resembling a bundle of linty blankets, slept beneath the statue of William Ellery Channing.

"I think we're more than a collection of cells. You can't dissect a soul or a personality, but it's there." Then she began dissecting the Mingo House board of trustees. There were factions, the people loyal to the ways of the old guard, like Nadia Gulbenkian, for example, and Rudy Schmitz's people, especially the young software executive, Jon Kim.

That day, Genevieve brought me to Clara Mingo's bedroom, showing me her brush and comb set, monogrammed and engraved with doves of peace. One of Clara's maids swore she saw the brush take flight to follow its owner to the first floor.

"The maid was deep in the cooking sherry that day," I said.

Genevieve called my attention to the ebony table, inlaid with mother-of-pearl, which Clara had used when conducting her séances. It had reverberated with the rapping of the departed, with spirits from her own family and shades of Civil War soldiers, two mayors of Boston, and Abraham Lincoln himself. Clara's afterlife was racially integrated, since "colored troops" from Robert Gould Shaw's 54th Massachusetts regiment marched here to speak. Then, scandalously, Clara dared summon the ghost of the Reverend Asa Lawrence Fowle of Trinity Church, Copley Square. That was too much for proper Bostonians; they knew Asa Fowle would have shunned Clara Mingo, whether he was dead or alive. So the family was consigned to social Siberia.

"That's when Corinth One really put his foot down. He ordered a Congregational minister to come and more or less exorcize the place. I think Corinth paid a priest to sprinkle the house with holy water too. He wanted to cover all the bases."

So Clara took the waters at various German spas, and when she and Corinth One returned, she became a respectable recluse, doing non-controversial embroidery for the poor and becoming an early advocate for the prevention of cruelty to animals. "She paid for a lot of drinking troughs for work horses all throughout Boston. The last one was on the Esplanade. It was vandalized by some idiots ten years ago. It had a bas-relief of Clara's favorite pony. I think the Museum of Fine Arts may have gotten what was left of it. August Saint-Gaudens supposedly designed it. But if he did, it wasn't his best work."

I peered beneath the table, which seemed to be Indian, judging by its carving, and discovered no levers, cranks, or cables to simulate ghosts.

"Clara wasn't a fraud. She really believed she was a medium."
"But her husband didn't. Obviously."
"He was a businessman. Whose business was death."
"So was hers."
"Touché. Sort of."

Chapter Three

Over the course of my weeks of shadowing Genevieve, I met the trustees one by one, as they dropped by Mingo House during the hours when docents gave tours. I was startled by how few there were: a mere five. Then, finally, the chaos of their commitments subsided, and a meeting was scheduled one humid Thursday evening.

I was the first trustee to arrive. I found Genevieve and Dorothea Jakes, another older docent from Wellesley, lugging something naked and flesh-colored down the staircase.

"Don't be alarmed," Dorothea laughed. "It's only 'Maude.'"

"It's a mannequin. From a department store," Genevieve said.

"We got it when Jordan Marsh closed." Dorothea was gasping a bit, but shooed away my offer to help. "Eventually, she'll be clothed…and sitting…at the dining room table."

"Maude" was thin and resembled Audrey Hepburn in *Roman Holiday*. Genevieve and Dorothea draped her in an old sheet and propped her in the front hall by the coat-rack.

"We don't want her to startle the ghosts," said Dorothea.

"Do you have any?" I asked.

"Clara Mingo thought so," Genevieve reminded me.

Nadia Gulbenkian, the senior member of the board in both age and years of service, arrived just as we were laughing because the sheet had slipped from the mannequin. "Terrible, terrible," Nadia was muttering. She was a dark woman in her vigorous sixties, with the suggestion of a moustache above her upper lip and the air of a person living in a state of perpetual blitzkrieg. Her late husband had been a political science professor at Harvard and the author of several books about the Cold War and McCarthyism, and Nadia was often a delegate to the Democratic national convention. She had served on the Mingo House board of trustees for a good decade, but tonight she seemed especially upset, her face flushed, her gray hair rebelling against the tortoiseshell combs supposed to tame it. "It's the roof over our heads," she said. She threw down her heavy faux-alligator pocketbook onto the vulnerable table by the door, disrupting the neat piles of brochures. "This board is going to have to act instead of pontificate. And we do not have a lot of time."

Then she rummaged through her pocketbook, taking out a crossword puzzle clipped from some newspaper, an English-Italian paperback dictionary, two tortoiseshell compacts, and a tube of Rollos before finding what she wanted. "It's the report from the architects, on the structural state of the roof. In a word, it's unsound, dangerous or close to it." She waved the document in her heavily veined hand. "Mingo House is doomed. To think this collection has survived intact for all these years and now, *because of carpentry*, it just may vanish."

Then Rudy Schmitz, the chairman of the board, sauntered in. He was a thin man with a salt-and-pepper ponytail and a face desiccated in a patrician way. He cultivated the air of a Brahmin progressive, but was neither. A native of Baltimore, he'd come north for college, then become a real estate broker before accumulating the capital to found some of the city's toniest businesses, including Flex, the gym with mirrored walls and a sushi bar, and Chill, the gelato place on Charles Street. He lived, I was told, in a lavish spread on Beacon Hill.

He was eating lemon sorbet from a cup emblazoned with the distinctive Chill logo, the Leaning Tower of Pisa wearing earmuffs. He knew perfectly well that all food and drink was banned from Mingo House but was chuckling at his little transgression. "Sorbet is mostly water. It doesn't have the fat content of dairy, so it won't stain. And I'm almost done." He had scant awareness of other people's feelings: "That's a lovely dress you're wearing, Nadia. You're looking extra chipper tonight."

Nadia seemed to be the type who would have scolded him about the sorbet but she had bigger things on her mind. "The roof is a disaster waiting to happen." She thrust a copy of the architects' report at Rudy. "Read it and weep." Instead of doing either, Rudy turned toward the eavesdropping docents. "Thank you as always. You may go now." Genevieve spoke up. "I've made the usual arrangements for rain upstairs," she told Nadia. "It looks pretty black over Cambridge." Nadia nodded and Genevieve opened the front door, revealing a sky in which thunderheads were multiplying. As Genevieve and Dorothea left, the remainder of the trustees came trudging in: Jon Kim, a dapper software executive from Cambridge; and Sean Ahearn, the vice president of a hospital in Somerville.

We were meeting at the rear of the house, on the first floor, in the dining room, which, as always, was set for a dinner that would never take place. A round mahogany table was covered by gilt-edged, raspberry pink-china and bewildering silverware only Victorians would comprehend, odd little forks, threatening spoons... Everything in the room seemed breakable, from the mirrors with their spiky gilt flowers to the score of figurines crowding every flat surface, the Meissen peasants minding sheep, milking cows, depositing a newly caught perch into a basket... I pressed my briefcase against my chest, so as not to swing it and shatter some artifact, as I made my way to the circle of metal chairs positioned near the windows for our meeting. A painting of three solemn girls—all lace and blonde ringlets, clustered around a chocolate-colored Newfoundland dog—seemed to stand sentinel behind us.

"Welcome to your first official meeting of the board of trustees of Mingo House, Mark," Rudy said, squeezing my bicep and holding the muscle a few seconds too long. "We may need a little comic relief. As well as your perspective about working with the media. I've told your fellow trustees all about your advertising expertise. Your Clio Awards. Etcetera."

From her pocketbook Nadia extracted four more copies of the architects' report. Mine, like the others I saw, was smeared with streaks of a fragrant and no doubt costly face powder. "To give you the executive summary, we need a new roof. In fact, the report stresses that the entire 'envelope' of the building is in question, structurally."

Various people sighed. Jon Kim emitted a long, low whistle. He was hard not to notice: he had a handsome face sculpted with high cheekbones, linebackers' shoulders, and a suit so tailored it might have been sprayed on. "Wow. And I mean wow," he said.

The estimates for the work of roof men, plasterers, electricians, pushed the cost to over $200,000.

"It's a tragedy, a tragedy pure and simple." Nadia had taken the Rollos out of her handbag and was putting several into her mouth, which was large and emphasized by a coating of caked scarlet lipstick. Looking in her direction, Rudy gave a stage sigh as if he wished that the troublesome roof and the troubled trustee might both be gone. "We have some serious fundraising to do. We can kick that off with the big party in August." He glanced in my direction. "And Mark can help us with some serious grant-writing."

"Won't the city just close us down? Aren't we endangering the public, just permitting people on the premises?" Jon Kim asked.

Rudy laughed, displaying his nicotine-stained teeth. "Nadia, your fear is contagious. You're giving poor Jon a panic attack."

Jon Kim opened his obsidian-black laptop. "Couldn't we contact some surviving member of the Mingo family? To donate some funds? Is that a possibility? I'll Google 'Mingo'…"

"Forget it," Nadia said. I knew Jon had joined the board six months ago, and Nadia now treated him like the novice she thought he was. "The Mingoes are extinct. You'd need a medium to summon them."

Jon commenced to laugh, and then Nadia, her face rigid with rage, reached into her bag. For an instant, a small, shrill part of me thought she might draw out some sort of weapon. Instead, she took what proved to be a flask of honeysuckle toilet water and dabbed some onto the loose skin of her neck. "Sometimes I wonder why I remain on this board. Sometimes I wonder."

Clearly Rudy was restraining himself because Nadia's cut was aimed at him, at his "new regime": she was the last trustee recruited to the board by the previous chair, Burrage Hone, the late authority on colonial America and two-time winner of the Pulitzer Prize.

"The death of a cultural institution is not an occasion for frivolity. Mingo House means more than some club or restaurant that gradually loses its Zagat stars and expires."

Everyone recognized this as a reference to Rudy's one major failure, Tank, his gay bar by the harbor in South Boston. Its location was too remote for lazy clubbers to trek, so it had lived up to its name in less than a year.

Hugging his laptop, Jon Kim rallied to Rudy's defense. "Nadia, that was uncalled for. Rudy brings some much-needed business acumen to this board. And knowledge of the consumer taste, local and national. Not to mention a cool head."

To my surprise, Rudy squeezed Jon's arm just as erotically as he'd squeezed mine, and as far as I knew Jon was married and straight. He wore a heavy gold wedding ring.

"Remember, Nadia, we're the trustees of Mingo House, charged with its care and capable of providing it. Throwing up our hands at every crisis that comes our way is hardly what Corinth Two would have hoped for when he gave this museum to the people of Boston and the world." Rudy was quoting some rhetoric from the brochure visitors received when they paid the docents for a tour. Nadia, long ago, had helped write this brochure, and her own words seemed to calm her.

Just then, a great crack of thunder, like a cliff slide in a quarry rent by dynamite, resounded, and rain came seething down. Nadia gazed almost fondly at the tall windows behind us, seemingly pleased by the wrath of nature. "Why don't we take a little walk upstairs, to assess the situation in the library? Why don't we see things first-hand?" Yanking her pocketbook from the floor, she stood and led the group away from the hesitating Rudy, who was the last to follow.

We trudged up the staircase. Just for conversation, I asked Rudy, "Who are those three girls in that painting in the dining room?"

"Oh, Aginesse, Alva, and Araminta, the triplets—Corinth Two's sisters who all died from complications of diphtheria. That really undid poor Clara."

"The Mingoes were kind of a hard-luck crew."

"Well, Clara felt cursed because of the money the family made during the Civil War. Manufacturing firearms." Rudy quickly tickled my nape. "Silly isn't it? Were we supposed to defeat the Confederacy with slingshots?"

As we reached the top floor, we could hear an ominous dripping. Sure enough, someone had assembled a potpourri of containers—wastebaskets, pails, some cooking pans, and plastic tubs—to catch the steady drip of water assaulting the library from its ceiling.

"Genevieve, the docent, the Shawmut College student, knows this building intimately. She knows exactly where to put the containers." The ceiling was moist with rivulets of water and appeared ready to break open like a piñata.

Jon Kim was sheltering his laptop under one arm. "This is worrisome. This is worrisome. We can't let this go. We've got to be proactive."

"Proactive?" Nadia scoffed. "The time to be proactive was five years ago, Jon. Long before you came on board."

"Let's not trade recriminations, Nadia." A drop hit Rudy on his shoulder. Nadia nudged him aside, and, from behind the red velvet sofa that had so many rips and tears it seemed to be molting, she dragged yet another wastebasket, one someone must have brought to Mingo House specifically for this purpose, since it was circumvented with a map of the world, a schoolchild's battered cast-off. Nadia aligned the wastebasket with the latest leak, and, in the process, again bumped against both Rudy and Jon Kim. Rudy was frowning at the various receptacles; he seemed worried that they marred the décor.

"Of course the first thing we need in this process is a record." From her bag, Nadia retrieved a digital camera and began photographing the ceiling, the pans, the monsoon outside.

Rudy kept chuckling. "I swear, Nadia, some day you're going to pull old Corinth Two himself out of that bag."

No one else joined him in his mirth.

Chapter Four

We were supposed to read the architects' report as soon as possible and meet the following Monday at Mingo House, having each written a list of possible responses. At this next meeting, an architect from Glidden & Associates would speak about their findings in greater detail.

On Sunday, I received a second late-night call, but this caller, unlike Rudy Schmitz, at least apologized. "Mark, it's Genevieve, Genevieve Courson from Mingo House. Please pardon the intrusion, especially at this hour, but I need a small favor. I'd like to show you a little something from school. Related to my internship." She hesitated. "I mean, you're a writer."

I tried unsuccessfully to censor my yawn. "...Okay."

"Come by Mingo House early, before the trustees' meeting tomorrow. Come at six-fifteen. Dorothea is off. She's at a wedding in Edgartown, so I'm manning the fort. I'll be there late."

I nodded, and then realized sleepily that she couldn't see me. "Sure. No problem."

"Was that Rudolph the Red-Nosed Reindeer?" Roberto said, in a perfect imitation of Rudy's voice, which he had experienced only via voice-mail.

"No. Just that ditzy docent."

I spent the next afternoon on our balcony, writing fresh material for my standup act. It was a warm, pollen-filled day, so, unusually for me, I consumed a couple of beers along with my salmon-burger and spinach and endive salad. By the time I changed into business attire, I had a subtle buzz.

I pushed open the front door to Mingo House. No lights were burning, so the rooms were shadowed, blurry. I realized then that there was a window thrown open toward the rear of the house because a humid breeze was trespassing through the rooms.

"Hello... Is anyone here?"

I saw the walnut staircase ascending to my left, and, at its base, on a plinth, the marble bust of Corinth Hollis Mingo, like something summoned during one of Clara's séances. On a shelf in the dining room, a Bohemian glass decanter glowed red as a vial of freshly drawn blood, and, nearby, at the dining room table, sat the mannequin—now fitted with something lavish, a dress, a ball gown, made of celadon-green bunched silk. Had they gotten a grant to buy some period clothing?

The floor creaked as I walked down the hall. Then, in the dining room, I detected a scent, something differing from the odor of dusty velvet or Oriental rugs; it was a modern perfume, one I remembered from a sample card bound into an issue of *Vanity Fair*.

The perfume seemed to be emanating from the mannequin, whose plaster features had become detailed, but not lifelike— there was no life in those liquid brown eyes, in the corpse in Victorian dress, slumped in the rosewood rocker.

For an instant, I couldn't move. I felt bolted to the spot beneath the portrait of the doomed Mingo triplets.

"Genevieve!" I said, knowing a response was out of the question.

Then I ran from Mingo House as fast as I could.

Chapter Five

She became known throughout the country, indeed, throughout the world. It was a slow news month, that May, and the media seized upon her murder the way a starving mutt seizes a piece of gristle—with greed, desperation, and tenacity.

Genevieve Courson, the college student I knew, became the "Victorian Girl" to the great public. She was the coed strangled, stripped, and then decked out in period dress—in a corset and lace mittens, in a chemise and button shoes, in a green dress with a great cabbage of a bustle, so fashionable during the 1880s. She had been pulled back in time to the decade of the Garfield assassination and Jack the Ripper. Mingo House had indeed "claimed" her. She was one with Aginesse, Alva, and Araminta.

Reporters from *USA Today* and *Paris-Match*, from the *New York Times* and the *Daily Mail*, besieged Mingo House. Camera crews filmed the "memorial" obstructing the front steps, the votive candles and poems on pink stationery, the plush puppies and daisies from Stop & Shop, the artificial roses and genuine grief scrawled across sympathy cards depicting sunsets, saints—and, most poignantly for me, swans.

We trustees couldn't meet at Mingo House without being interviewed, so we convened at the Ritz bar and drafted a brief, curt statement to the press, saying as little as possible, of course. Long despairing that Mingo House would ever be noticed, its trustees were now paralyzed by this veritable hurricane of publicity.

The police interviewed us all, most doggedly, me. I told them everything I knew, including about Genevieve's late night request, but the "little something from school" that she'd mentioned she wanted to give me was not, to my knowledge, found at the crime scene. "Maude," as naked as the day she was manufactured, was left unmolested under her sheet, where Genevieve and Dorothea had placed her—while Genevieve's street clothes had presumably been stolen. Nothing else in Mingo House was so much as touched.

What did I know about Genevieve Courson, beyond that she was a docent on a volunteer basis and a student at Shawmut College, a few blocks down Beacon Street toward Mass Ave? True, I had been with her for two days per week for almost a month. She was very talkative, one of those young people who seem to find themselves endlessly fascinating, but when I reviewed the conversations I'd had with her, I realized she'd revealed very little about her life. Every lunch hour she'd ordered the same spicy vegan burrito with extra guacamole and a Pepsi. She was a fan of German expressionist cinema ("I had boyfriend I nicknamed Nosferatu"). She ransacked thrift shops for "relics" as she called them: a quilted bed-jacket of silver lame, bracelets of bright bakelite fruit, pins encrusted with rhinestones, and her favorites, cameos—of shell, agate, and celluloid. She would purchase these things on her lunch hour and return breathlessly to show us each one. She bought these with more than a nod to retro chic; she was focused on the history, the context, of every item. "This is a little bit of the past, a bygone era. The people are gone, but their handiwork survives."

She had expressed a desire to live in the past. "Not for long. Maybe just for a day. Long enough to see what it's like."

But she shied away from specifics about herself and I never pressed her. "I'm from north of Boston," she would reply, when asked about her origins. "I'm still deciding," she would answer, when asked to name her major. About graduate school or her goals in life she would say, "I'm sort of making it up as I go along."

But she was a marvelous docent because she truly seemed to love Mingo House. She would run her finger along the creamy Carrara marble of a mantle and say, "Imagine, this stone came over on a steamer with a paddle wheel, across the Atlantic." The color of the brownstone reminded her of fruitcake. "It's like this house is a recipe handed down, perfectly preserved, to us. It's a gift. How many people really appreciate that?"

She had an essence I found attractive. And I believe she liked me. Who had so disliked her as to kill her? Who indeed could strangle a college girl, keep the pressure on her neck while she shuddered and gasped and lost consciousness during those endless seconds? Who could plan this intricate kind of crime? Someone with a passion that had curdled into anger, a boyfriend or an ex-boyfriend? But what did the clothing and setting suggest? That the Victorian era or what it symbolized held a potent attraction—or repulsion—for the killer?

No signs of struggle were found at Mingo House. Nothing in the dining room—the raspberry-pink china, the Meissen peasants, the portrait of the three doomed children—had been shoved or shattered. The killer had been brutal with the victim but tender with the artifacts. Perhaps Genevieve had been murdered elsewhere and then transported to Mingo House.

Finding or creating the period-style dress—it was a reproduction, which the media insisted fit perfectly—suggested weeks of planning. Had Genevieve sat for fittings, with a tailor, or with a tailor and her killer, as she was measured?

Chapter Six

Roberto had become an excellent cook, as gauged by our slightly expanded waistlines. He was placing jumbo-sized shrimp he'd marinated in lime juice atop a grill on our balcony. He was also nervously watching for Miriam Hilliard, our friend and neighbor, sure she would reproach him for this violation of condominium rules. "Thou shall not barbecue," he was laughing. "And shellfish to boot." He came from a family of Puerto Rican Jews.

Miriam was the reason we could afford this costly address. She had inherited what was an immense unit from a cousin who'd bought the condominium as an investment—and then subdivided it, offering us the resulting small unit for a flagrantly generous price. It was a reward, literally, for our saving her daughter, Chloe, from a psychotic who'd seized her in an inheritance scheme on Cape Cod.

Chloe, now a precocious student at a Back Bay girls' school, had smelled the mesquite charcoal and came running onto her balcony, adjoining ours. "Mother alert, Mother alert! The Mothership will return in twenty minutes."

"The shrimp are almost done." Roberto prodded them with a fork. "Where is she?"

"She went to buy freshwater pearls. She's making a bracelet to donate to the Channel 2 auction."

That was our local PBS fundraiser. "Isn't she a little late? Hasn't that already started?"

"Yeah, she's having a cow. The pearls came late because some parasite was croaking all the mussels on the farm…" She paused to chew another gummy worm. "Hey, how about that weird murder? With that girl dressed up like she was dating Sherlock Holmes. Mark, didn't that happen where you work on the board of trustees?"

I tried not to blanch but was sure Chloe had seen me; she didn't miss much. No one but Roberto knew I'd found Genevieve Courson's body. The police had withheld that from the media.

Roberto removed the shrimp from the grill, doused the charcoal with water meant for our impatiens, and sprayed the air with a citrus-scented freshener that did nothing to disguise his cloud of gourmet smog.

"How about we forget about it? All of us. We've had trouble enough without looking for more." He gave me a look that could have grilled me too.

Chapter Seven

But, somehow, I wanted to commemorate the young woman I knew, rescue her, in my mind, from the lurid screenplay the media were fabricating. I wanted to attend any funeral or memorial service scheduled. So I stopped by Shawmut College, which occupied a series of brownstones not unlike Mingo House itself, but much altered. Television crews from Channel 7 and Fox News had parked their trucks in the neighborhood, and I recognized Marcia Haight, one of Boston's star anchors, interviewing a group of young people outside a fraternity. My goal, luckily, was in the other direction.

The college registrar's office retained vestiges of its origins as a private men's club: egg-and-dart molding, mosaic lions on the floor. The counter was manned by a plump woman with the kind of baby-soft skin that doesn't wrinkle with age.

"I'm trying to find out about the funeral plans for one of your students, a young woman I knew, Genevieve Courson."

"Are you from the media?"

"No."

"Show me your credentials."

"I'm not a reporter. I volunteer at Mingo House. Genevieve... was such a great person. She had an internship there, as a docent. We spent quite a bit of time together. She was a remarkable person."

The woman's expression softened instantaneously. "Oh, what a shock. What a crime. So senseless."

At first she hesitated to speak, checking the room to make sure her colleagues weren't listening. "She was always so polite. Only the good die young."

At this point a student interrupted the conversation. "I need some help." She shifted her shoulders and her backpack, which bore a patch advocating the legalization of marijuana. "I've decided to drop 'Aspects of Government'."

"You must inform your professor first, miss. As a common courtesy."

"But why?"

"It's policy."

The sternness returned to her face but left as the girl strode away. "Genevieve was nothing like that."

"You knew her personally?"

She leaned over the counter. "Genevieve had trouble paying her bills. She had to drop some courses because she couldn't afford the tuition. The poor kid. And she was smart as a whip. I really felt for her, who wouldn't? But then, this spring, she said some money was coming through. I really thought things were looking up."

"Money? She never mentioned that." Yet something financed her thrift shop spending sprees.

"She was very modest about it. Never one to put on airs. Like that spoiled brat who just left: 'My father owns a car dealership, so I'm royalty.'"

"So Genevieve had come into some money? Was it a lot?"

The woman, whose badge informed me her name was Trudie, leaned so close I could smell her clove Life Saver. "She confided in me. She said, 'I'm fixed financially for a while.' And now dead. God love her."

Then the spoiled brat returned and cast off her backpack onto the counter. "I'm tired of being given the runaround," she snapped. "I pay tuition here, and I expect some service." I wanted to get Genevieve Courson's home address and telephone number, but now wasn't the time. "Genevieve lived in Howard

Hall until last year. Her best friend was Peggy O'Connell," Trudie called as I left.

The dormitory was a block farther toward Mass Ave, a hideous building of steel, glass, and sparkly beige brick that must have replaced something Victorian that burnt; it had been put up before historic preservation guidelines were in vogue. It was co-ed, but with post 9/11 security in effect, impossible for me to penetrate. Instead I stood helpless under the magnolias blossoming by the entrance. There, a red-headed young man in a Patriots T-shirt accosted me. "You have 'reporter' written all over you. Haven't you exploited this story enough?"

I challenged him. "What story?"

"Gimme a break." He might have been considered handsome, except that his features were too large for his face. He was heavily freckled, muscular, and peeved. "You're here about Genevieve, aren't you?"

Something made me defiant and a little daring. "I found her body."

He flinched, lost his composure for a moment. "So what do you want?"

"Look, I'm not from the media. I work at Mingo House. I knew Genevieve, I liked her. I want to find out if there's a funeral happening… Were you a close friend?"

He was chewing gum discreetly, using his back molars. "Peggy O'Connell was her roommate. She lives in Howard 201."

"I'm just wondering whether there will be a service or a funeral, anything open to the public."

"Genevieve was a very private person." He had no problem assigning her to the past tense this soon. He rocked gently back and forth on his expensive sneakers, which were emblazoned with silver cheetahs and endorsed by a big basketball star.

I decided to lie a little. "She mentioned an old boyfriend who was giving her trouble. She'd nicknamed him Nosferatu." I wanted to say, It wasn't you, was it?

He stopped rocking and just stared. "She hadn't dated anyone since the accident."

"What accident?"

"She was injured last year, in a motorcycle crash. That idiot Zack Meecham drove them both into a tree. She was limping around for months. Hey, I have to get going." He was jiggling one hairy, muscular leg. He had the calves of a runner. He was the sort who wore shorts the moment the calendar dared announce it was spring, even if the forsythia was still embedded in ice.

"Go in." To my surprise, he climbed the steps to the dormitory, inserted a plastic card into a slot and held the buzzing door open for me to enter. "Go see Peggy O'Connell in Room 201."

"I'm Mark Winslow. Thanks."

"Fletcher Coombs."

Room 201 was open, allowing the soft sounds of classical music into the hall. The room was hung with bolts of Balinese batik and posters of Venice, U2, and, of all things, Friedrich Nietzsche. On one wall, a series of shelves held a collection of unicorns, in resin, bisque, and pewter, some with glitter sprinkled on their horns. A heavyset girl with auburn hair was leaning on some pillows on the floor in a corner, at work on a book of sudoku. She spoke first. "Hello. I don't give *interviews*. I don't care to speak to any more reporters about poor Genevieve. If you have any questions, I suggest you contact the police."

"I'm not a reporter, I promise." I stepped inside without being invited. The room was a double but with one bed, at the far left, stripped, and one desk equally barren. "I worked with Genevieve at Mingo House. We ate lunches together and hit the thrift shops. I was actually the person...who found her."

She stopped doing her sudoku. She indicated a squishy blob of a chair. "How awful for you. How awful for all of us."

I sat.

"Genevieve was such a sweet person. She wouldn't hurt a fly. Wouldn't *have*."

I said I wanted to know of any service that was happening, as did "her friends" at Mingo House. She seemed to be assessing my trustworthiness. "Do you have any idea who could have done such a thing? Did Genevieve have any enemies, any former boyfriends who were bothering her?"

"Did she ever." She replaced the classical CD with Green Day. "That idiot Zack who almost killed her on the Jamaicaway. In the motorcycle crash. Her leg was torn up, it was hideous." Perhaps that was why Genevieve favored peasant dresses and vintage clothing—the lower hemlines.

I would wait for her to confirm the name. "Zack…?"

"Zack Meecham."

"Has he bothered her lately?"

"Not at all." She actually smiled. "He's dead, he was killed in the accident. Oak tree one, Zack zero. It's horrible to say, but that was one of the best things that happened to her—Zack checking out." She continued, how Zack had been insulting, controlling, condescending. He was a graduate student at Harvard. They had met when she taking a course at the Extension School. At first he seemed a mentor of sorts. "But then he became totally toxic. I mean he was a regular Superfund site, they should have put him on an EPA hit list. He tried to take over her life. She almost went to the police."

"So why was she riding on his motorcycle? If she considered him a dangerous man, that seems like a dangerous thing to do."

"They had been to a party. She needed a ride home, to the dorm. He was the only person left who was sober. She needed her sleep. She had exams the next day."

Peggy was the robust type who plays field hockey or maybe softball, with an intelligence that made me want to earn her respect.

"How did it happen?"

"He swerved to avoid a jaywalker. It was on a bad curve. He slammed into a tree and died instantly. Her leg was a mess."

"It's so awful, her surviving all that—"

"And then this horrible thing."

She set down her book of sudoku. "Why do you think she was murdered *at Mingo House*?"

"I have no idea." But that wasn't quite true. Mingo House had somehow figured in her death. Was it tied somehow to the "little something for school," the project? Probably not.

"Why was she killed there and dressed that way?" She was glancing at the collection of unicorns when she added, "It's perverse."

Perverse, yes, exactly the word. "This Zack. He was much older?"

She stood and took a neat stack of books from her desk. "I've got a final coming up." She focused on my eyes with an opthamologist's precision. "Why are you doing this? This investigation? Were you in love with her too?"

It was a bold question, but a sound one. I'd gotten in life-threatening trouble before, and of my own volition. "There was something compelling about her… We had a kind of connection. Nothing sexual."

"Yeah," she said. "You're probably gay."

Why, for a moment, was I insulted? I didn't respond.

"She had every straight guy panting after her."

The books under her arm were all about philosophy, Hegel and Kant. She had the manner of a much older person, a confidence few college students could muster. "I'll tell you something, and I feel guilty about saying this, but Genevieve was trouble. She just seemed to attract trouble. Right until the end."

Like the Mingoes, I thought. And don't all murder victims "attract trouble," somehow, by definition?

Ushering me out of the room, she joined a group of students, including Fletcher Coombs, chattering in the echoing stairwell.

That evening, Roberto and I ate with Miriam and Chloe on the terrace of their condominium next door. Miriam was now a strict vegetarian but Chloe was a confirmed carnivore. "And she likes red meat only," Miriam complained. "I mean beef is the whole reason we're deforesting the Amazon. We're razing the rain forest to create pastures for cattle. Nature is being destroyed for the sake of cheeseburgers. Some tradeoff."

Chloe and Roberto were slathering their medium-rare burgers with Miriam's home-made onion relish, which was delicious—spicy, starting a five-alarm fire in your mouth. To appease our hostess, I'd agreed to have the curried tofu with snap peas she had cooked for herself.

"What was that girl like?" Chloe asked as Miriam and Roberto frowned in tandem. They knew Chloe meant Genevieve Courson.

"We're letting the police handle that situation, aren't we?" When Miriam used the "royal we," she meant business.

Chloe was wolfing down her hamburger and gulping her glass of Trader Joe's limeade. "I don't get it. Why would the killer dress her in Victorian clothing? It doesn't make sense. It takes too much time. A killer would want quick, right? Just surprise, kill, then leave. Maybe she dressed *herself.*"

No-one—from the police, the media, or the Mingo House staff—had suggested that. Everyone had assumed the clothing on Genevieve was some kind of fetish, some ritual or "signature."

"It's the end of the school year. She might have been going to a party. Or a prom." Mugging, onion relish on her chin, Chloe regressed and again became a little girl.

Miriam began ladling tofu onto Chloe's plate.

"Mum, it tastes like Styrofoam. It…is…so…gross." (Chloe was right.)

"They don't have proms in college," Miriam said. "And no one goes to a prom wearing a bustle."

"But I'll bet the students had costume parties, if not in May then at Halloween. She could have designed that dress for a class." Stupidly, I said it out loud: "I should research whether she was enrolled in any costume-design classes."

"You'll do nothing of the sort." Roberto was also wearing relish on his chin, but I didn't dare mention it now. "Mark, if you play Hercule Poirot again, it will have *consequence*s for us."

"The last thing we need is another murderer in our lives." Miriam refreshed her limeade.

Chloe emitted a gentle burp. "What if we already have one but we just don't know it?"

Chapter Eight

The next morning's *Globe* included a notice stating that Genevieve Courson's funeral would be held the following morning at ten at the Cafferty/McGinn Funeral Home in Lynn, a former mill town north of Boston. I was just tearing out the notice when someone began knocking delicately at our condominium door, fluttering their fingers against the wood, making the sound of a small bird trapped in a box. It was Chloe, waving the very same obituary page and whispering, "Her funeral is tomorrow. Is Roberto out? Good. The Mothership is delivering that bracelet to WGBH. Oh, you already saw it. You *are* taking this seriously."

Her butter-yellow dress, of some filmy material, billowed as she fidgeted. "Are you going? May I come?"

"Yeah, your mom and Roberto would love that. There'd be World War Three *and* a divorce."

She was chewing a mouthful of Swedish fish, which made it impossible for me to understand her response.

"What?"

She swallowed the red candy and licked her lips. "Like that's stopped you before."

"I almost got killed.'

"But you saved my life." Her face was expectant, guarded, hopeful.

"Thank God." She enveloped me in her spindly arms.

So I drove up to Lynn, in the one suit I owned (wrinkled and in need of dry cleaning), a salsa-spotted tie, and scuffed wing tips, all dating from my years in advertising. The funeral home was a one-story structure of dun-colored brick, incongruous in a neighborhood of sagging three-decker houses covered in blistered paint or dented aluminum siding. Directly across the street, half of the funeral home's parking lot had been commandeered by media trucks and reporters practicing their commentary into microphones: "Doug, it's a somber scene here in Lynn…" Wooden barricades separated this mob from any mourners arriving.

"Sir? Do you have a moment?"

"Are you a family member? How are you feeling?"

"What did Genevieve Courson mean to you?"

Silent, I reached the safety of the funeral home porch, where, under a maroon canvas canopy, the somber male staff greeted me, their bouncers' physiques at odds with the delicate way they clasped their hands and covered their crotches.

Inside, everything in the hallway was beige: the carpeting, the wallpaper, and the shades of the brass lamps. Two surprises hit me next: the sight of Genevieve in her open casket, and the rows of empty chairs, each a rebuke. We were the only two "people" at the service. The media/mourner ratio was about three-hundred to one.

Signing the condolence book open on the maple lectern, I noted three other names in the lines above mine. I felt guilty, signing and confirming my presence here, violating the wishes of my partner and best friend, and, of course, linking myself publicly with this case and perhaps arousing the suspicions of the police. As I placed the pen back next to the page, I felt a bulky presence to my right. It was Fletcher Coombs, whose freckles seemed to have faded with stress.

I had to say it. "Where is everybody?" Unfortunately, it came out sounding flippant.

"Are you done? Because I'd like to sign… I certainly hope people won't come just out of curiosity."

Was that a dig at me? He seemed chill as the corpses in the funeral home freezer, in his tie with little New England Patriots insignia, which I found a bit inappropriate. An elderly couple materialized behind him, so I fled to a seat in the anonymous middle of the room.

Genevieve was posed in suit of peat-brown wool that seemed alien to her wardrobe and personality. The ring that normally adorned her nose had been removed and the henna had been shampooed from her hair. The frilly collar of her custard-yellow blouse concealed any ligature marks left by her strangler. She resembled a prim young secretary from the early 1960s. Draped across the gray metal casket was a blanket of roses, so moist and white they looked made of cold cream. There were no other arrangements here, nothing.

I counted five people in the room: Fletcher, the elderly couple, a woman in a purple leather jacket, and Dorothea Jakes. Then Nadia, of all people, came lumbering in, almost chic in a lilac tweed suit. What was she doing here? I had thought she saw Genevieve as a necessary nuisance back at Mingo House, conscientious but not terribly serious.

Then the canned organ music, which had been droning faithfully in the background, ceased, as a minister, together with an older man with Genevieve's sharp distinctive nose and the contours of her skull, proceeded up the aisle. This was, I assumed, her father, for, when he reached the front row of seats, he broke free of the minister's arm, and, approaching the casket, tenderly touched the dead girl's forehead in a soothing gesture. Then he wiped his eyes with a very large handkerchief, and sat down, alone, in a chair in the first row.

"We gather here to remember a life that while brief was extraordinary and touched so many..." Clearly the minister wasn't making up his eulogy spontaneously; he said nothing about the sparse house. He continued, offering no special insights into Genevieve's life; she was a devoted daughter and a loyal friend. Only toward the end of his tribute did he allow the horror of her death to intrude into this beige, embalmed setting: "Some twisted soul, some sad and lost individual, callously and violently ended her life, but he did nothing to sully the wonderful young woman she actually was." The "actually" was odd. Then he read some obscure psalms and the service was over. According to the felt board with white plastic letters posted above the condolence book, Genevieve was going to be cremated, so there would be no procession to a grave.

"Are you going back to the house?" the elderly couple was asking the woman in the purple leather jacket. "Oh, I'm not going *there*," the woman all but snapped.

None of the mourners spoke to Mr. Courson, but crept away with the discretion of shoplifters.

"Do you want a few minutes alone with your daughter?" asked one of the funeral home staff. Mr. Courson nodded.

Both Nadia and Dorothea Jakes had evaporated, so I stepped back into the hall, where I met Fletcher, studying an eighteenth-century engraving of a lily, one of those botanical prints people hang when their imagination fails.

Three more cops had come out of the woodwork. Boston police, I noticed, casing the place.

"Not many people from school."

He glanced at me and then back at the print. "It's exam time."

"But her father—"

"Her father has issues."

"Who were those others?"

"Neighbors. What's it to you?"

Just at that moment Mr. Courson emerged from his time with his daughter, but he was not alone. He was accompanied by a uniformed policeman who was telling him, "You can go to the crematorium, if you want, Larry. Don't let me cramp your style."

Was the policeman protecting Mr. Courson or guarding him? Could his "issues" be criminal?

"I'd just as soon head home." Mr. Courson almost lost his balance, but the cop caught him, steadying his shoulder. Then the pair of them veered slowly toward the exit, never to see Genevieve again.

Fletcher appeared more haggard than when we met at the condolence book. "I'm going to the house."

He was either inviting me along or saying this as a polite way to get rid of me. "May I follow you in my car?"

"I'll give you a lift."

"There are all those reporters."

"I've parked on a side street. We'll go out the back."

Marcia Haight, with her crew, awaited us. "This must be such a terrible shock…"

Then Fox News barreled up. "Hey, what's with the father? Is he a suspect?"

Fletcher and I ignored them. They gave up pursuing us when a funeral home hunk snapped, "Hey, shut up or take your sorry asses elsewhere."

Fletcher drove a battered olive-green SUV, its rear window dense with decals from national parks and with a line of dancing bears courtesy of the Grateful Dead. Inside, it was spotless, vacuumed but shabby. The only clutter, if it qualified as such, was an atlas of road maps of Massachusetts cities, a windshield scraper, and a Dunkin' Donuts insulated coffee mug. As before, Fletcher had an air of tension about him, a sullen formality understandable when someone close to you dies so shockingly.

"Are you a fan of the Dead?" That came out wrong.

"I inherited the car from my parents." He started the engine. His keys were on a chain along with a small enamel American flag.

He almost clipped a woman I recognized as a host on *Good Morning America*. He quickly lost one news truck trailing us by making turn after turn and speeding down several one-way streets the wrong way.

I wanted to get him talking, about Genevieve and her father. We were fresh from the service and they were the natural subject for conversation. In particular, I was wondering about Mr. Courson. "What was with the cop?"

"I told you, Mr. Courson has issues."

"Legal issues?"

"Big time." He kept his eyes on the road as we passed empty mill buildings where shoes had once been manufactured and then a sub shop, a potato chip factory, and a Baptist church for evangelical Hispanics.

I would wait for Fletcher to elaborate about the father. He was obviously the sort who resented questions. A blue Civic with duct tape mending its windshield cut us off at a green light and Fletcher exploded: "You dumb shit! Go back to where you came from!" He was well-built enough to win any fight not involving weapons. Gunning the engine, he seemed a little contrite. "It was kids."

"In the Civic?"

"No, with Genevieve's dad. He was accused of diddling a kid. He's a sex offender. He's under house arrest. He wears one of those ankle bracelets."

How awful, I thought, for her. What a burden for a young woman to carry. No wonder people had shunned Mr. Courson at the funeral. Especially if his crimes were recent. My sympathy for the man curdled with revulsion, so that the two emotions battled, spiders in a jar.

We turned right, and, to my surprise, the dilapidated houses gave way to woods and a small park with a baseball diamond—and then a street of freestanding single-family homes appeared, once-fine Greek revival structures with porches and proud Doric columns. We stopped at a house abutting a pewter-gray, rain-swollen pond.

"He lives in there. That's where Genevieve grew up."

A police car was parked at the curb. So was a truck from the Canadian Broadcasting Company.

"How is her dad doing?" I asked Fletcher.

"Not great. What do you expect?"

"Is it okay to visit?"

"Man, the water's gotten higher!"

He was right about that. It had flooded a garage and inundated a redwood picnic table twenty yards from the house.

The cop came out of the house just as we approached it. "Poor devil," he said to us. Which of those words did he mean more?

Fletcher rang the bell. Then Marcia Haight and her crew came climbing onto the porch, almost stumbling over a stack of firewood, elbowing the Canadians aside. "Who on earth could have killed Gen?" she asked us. Just then, the front door—still decorated with a Thanksgiving wreath of Indian corn—was pulled open to reveal Mr. Courson in his grief-black suit, now barefoot and holding a glass of clear liquid.

"Fletcher, I can always count on you. Thank you, thank you as always." They hugged. That was a surprise.

"I'm Mark Winslow. I knew Genevieve from the museum."

"Oh, that place. I'm Larry. Or what's left of me." His sigh turned into a deep sob. Fletcher patted his arm.

The interior of the house was beautiful, unexpected in this neighborhood. The wide floorboards gleamed with wax and the rooms were furnished with Victorian pieces that would not be out of place in Mingo House: a sofa carved with clusters of grapes, chairs upholstered in needlepoint and velvet. One whole wall was hung with daguerreotypes, portraits that could command formidable prices at auction. Mr. Courson apologized for having nothing to drink but birch beer, which he served us in elegant cut-glass tumblers. Fletcher joined me on the sofa in front of a low table stacked with books of photography: Cartier-Bresson, David Bailey, Richard Avedon.

"Mr. Courson is an incredible photographer." Fletcher began jiggling his right leg.

"*Was.*" Mr. Courson's tone was bitter. "That's all finished." He scratched his ankle, covered by his pants leg. Perhaps the bracelet was fastened on that leg.

"He had a studio downtown."

Mr. Courson blinked rapidly and sipped his soft drink.

"You stopped taking photographs? Why?" Just as my words took flight I guessed that photography was somehow related to his legal troubles.

"It was part of the entrapment. Part of the whole scam." Fletcher was one of those people who channel excess energy by wiggling one foot, and as soon as one became calm, the other activated. "There's this girl who has a screw loose who made a pass at Mr. Courson. When he said 'No way,' she made a federal case out of it. Then her parents got in on the act, and the whole thing snowballed."

"Times like these, you learn who your friends are. And who they aren't."

On the wall, contrasting to the daguerreotypes, were photographs of the girl who grew up to be Genevieve. Her young smile seemed heartbreakingly brave, given the fate that lay in ambush this spring. She was clutching a stuffed monkey, awash in tropical surf, riding a palomino pony through British-green meadows… These photographs suggested affluence and security, but this was no doubt before Mr. Courson was charged.

"Just a terrible thing. A terrible thing." Mr. Courson was talking about all that had befallen him.

"We all liked Genevieve at the museum." Again I had mentioned the site of the murder. I tried to amend things: "She had a wonderful rapport with the visitors."

"Except with the one who killed her." Mr. Courson put his birch beer onto the table with the books of photography. "I thought her problems were over when that crazy professor killed himself. And did the world a favor. Of course he almost killed my daughter in the act."

"Zack Meecham. He sure was a prize," Fletcher said.

I decided to ask questions while I could. "Was he…harassing her?"

"Genevieve was such an awesome person. Sweet, sincere, but kind of a creep magnet." Fletcher loosened his Patriots tie. His suit was quite preppie, from Brooks Brothers, perhaps.

"Who could have done such a thing?" Mr. Courson asked Fletcher, who was jiggling his left foot at the moment. He wore gold-buckled loafers instead of sneakers. He was self-assured and probably a little vain. I couldn't tell how bright he was. He and Genevieve had been more than classmates. Had they ever been "involved," or was he merely an old friend of the family? I would ask on the ride back to my car.

Fletcher stopped shaking both of his legs. "The police have a couple of suspects."

That was news to me and certainly not reported by the media.

"Suspects?" Mr. Courson knocked his knee against the table, almost upsetting his glass of birch beer onto a book, *The Secret Paris of the 30's* by Brassai. "Who are they?"

"People of interest. I don't know the details. You know, I have...sources."

This vague allusion seemed to soothe Mr. Courson, and, after Fletcher insisted, the bereaved man showed me the walls of the adjoining room, which were dazzling with his photographs: a Celtics game, eroded rocks and mosses, otters devouring starfish, Senator Ted Kennedy, the cliffs of Big Sur—and a single nude, a seated female with her shapely back to the camera and her buttocks not quite concealed by the strip of crimson silk beneath her. The nude jolted me because for an instant I thought—feared—it was Genevieve. "Fantastic."

Outside, the media had vanished. In the car, Fletcher seemed relieved that the visit was over. "I really feel for the guy, wow. I mean, he's lost his little girl. He's lost everything she used to be too." He stripped off his Patriots tie and rolled it neatly into his pocket.

"What did you mean that the police have some people of interest? Do you have...inside information?"

"Nah. I just said that to make him feel better."

Which hadn't worked. "Why did he believe you?"

"My dad's a cop."

"Really. Where?"

"Here in Lynn. Genevieve and I went to school here together. At St. Monica's. In City Hall Square. We bonded because neither of us was Catholic."

"Were you and Genevieve—?"

"Friends. We were just friends."

"And your dad is a fan of the Grateful Dead?"

"No, my mom. She once met Jerry Garcia. She's from San Francisco. They met in college at Northeastern."

Fletcher seemed to have taken a shorter route back because we had arrived at the funeral home parking lot in record time. By now poor Genevieve was being incinerated in a retort. "I appreciate the ride." As I set one wing-tip shoe onto the pavement, I asked, "What happened to Genevieve's mother? Was she at the service? Are they divorced?"

"She died of breast cancer two years ago. An incredibly sweet lady. Her photograph was on the wall—the nude, on the red silk." Then he reached across the passenger seat, and, clutching its handle, slammed the door shut and sped the SUV away.

Chapter Nine

The next morning, helping to remove some "memorial" items from the Mingo House steps and rub off a message marked in lipstick on the brownstone—"Genevieve Courson, forever in our hearts"—I was interrupted by Dorothea Jakes. In sunglasses and a blue-and-white seersucker dress, she was carrying a single peony. "Oh, I feel so gauche, but I was actually going to leave a flower in memory of Genevieve. To counter the presence of the Beanie Babies. You know Genevieve was a bit of a kook, but I enjoyed her. At times." Then, the usually diplomatic Dorothea blurted it out: "Wasn't that the most pathetic funeral?"

"Well, plenty of reporters came."

"But only two trustees. And I was so surprised Bryce Rossi wasn't there." She deposited her peony on the lowest step, next to a resin unicorn. Had Peggy O'Connell brought that figurine from her collection? She hadn't even gone to her room-mate's funeral.

"Who's Bryce Rossi?"

"Oh, he's a real character. He does genealogical research. He used to meet Genevieve some evenings."

"His nickname wasn't Nosferatu, was it? Was he an old boyfriend?"

She scoffed. "Hardly!" Then Dorothea gave me his business card, on thick teal cardboard, with embossed lettering reading: "Bryce Ralph Rossi, Appraisals & Genealogical Research." The card listed a Boston address in the financial district and a phone number with a city exchange.

I telephoned Bryce Rossi's business number, discovered it was disconnected, and then, via directory assistance, found him at a number in the South End, Boston's "gay ghetto." Bryce told me Genevieve Courson had consulted him about "some personal research." My subsequent questions were met with responses that became progressively more curt and opaque until he told me, "Look, you're a stranger. You're just a voice on the telephone. I mean, we've never even met…"

So I suggested we do exactly that, meet for a bite in the Back Bay. He insisted it be dinner, not lunch, and requested he pick out the restaurant.

Newbury Street that evening was thronged with people, mostly college-age or at least young, savoring the sunlight, the foreplay of summer. They ignored the "old" businesses: the Ritz and the sole merchant still devoted to fur, the galleries selling the American Impressionists. They passed the antique shops, their grated windows gleaming with cascades of pocket watches, with golden dryads hoisting aloft candles and crystal prisms, alabaster putti riding clouds and eating cherries, Lalique bowls frosted with prancing bathing beauties…They passed windows of ormolu girandoles, Lalique vases, and busts of French courte-sans—of terra-cotta the same papery gray of wasps' nests. They ignored the funky places Genevieve loved, with their racks of trash and treasures. These people—yuppies and rich college kids from Europe and Asia—swept into the open air cafes to eat tapas and spring rolls, to drink designer beer and apple martinis. They strolled cockily because this was Boston's *paseo*, thick with youth, status, and hormones.

Bryce Rossi was lean; any excess flesh anywhere on his body had been dieted or exercised away. Every hair on his head was perfectly cut and lay obediently in place without the burden of gel. He had an obsessive-compulsive neatness, and was, to me, totally sexless.

"There's so much to discuss." He chose a restaurant on Newbury Street called Villa D'Este, which had "al fresco dining." "It's me, Bryce Rossi," he told the maitre d', and then tried a few lines of Italian. His performance meant little to the staff, and we were given a corner table next to a small concrete cupid. "I spent a magnificent year in Padua, studying abroad. I find the whole Mediterranean world so simpatico. Healthier, more sensual." He reached across the table and ran his skeletal finger down the back of my hand.

The waiter saved me from having to respond. Judging by his flaxen hair and name tag ("Dmitri"), he was Slavic, which seemed to disturb my companion a great deal. "Isn't Luciano here tonight? He always knows exactly what I want. He can all but read my thoughts."

"He returned to Milan last January, sir."

"What about Mauritzio?" Bryce relished pronouncing these names with shameless Italian gusto.

"Mauritzio left a while back. He's working in a restaurant in Chicago."

Bryce gave a haughty snort. "Things certainly have changed."

"We're under new management."

"As I feared. But your wine list is still respectable, I trust?"

Before I could refuse any liquor whatsoever, Bryce had ordered a bottle of Palazzo Barbarini 1992, costing forty-eight dollars. "I know exactly what to have. Veal Umbria, you'll swoon." The vermillion dots on his tie seemed to move surreptitiously. He was the sort to hijack a conversation unless thwarted, so I made a preemptive strike: "Were you close to Genevieve?"

He leaned over the bread and extra virgin olive oil. "We were soul mates."

But surely not bed mates, I thought.

He dipped his heel of bread into the olive oil, pressed it, and thrust it into his thin-lipped mouth. "Genevieve had a passion for history. That we shared. She was a world-class researcher. Why she was enamored of that fool at Harvard, I never knew."

"Fool?"

"Zack Meecham. You didn't know him? Consider yourself blessed. What a fraud. He taught a course about post-Civil War America. She got permission to audit it. He was insufferable."

"Why?"

"Oh, please. Don't make me lose my appetite. Let's not bring him up unless we have insecticide handy. He makes my skin crawl."

"But he's…dead."

"Mercifully. He should have won a Darwin Award. Or perhaps we might give it to that tree on the Jamaicaway. I'm sorry, but I refuse to discuss him." Bryce had a prominent Adam's apple, and as he spoke, it was getting a workout, so he liberated it by unfastening the top button on his shirt.

"I warned Genevieve. But she was headstrong, as you must have observed."

The waiter brought the bottle of wine and expertly poured us each a glass. Bryce sipped. "Magnificent? Don't you agree? Good heavens! Don't guzzle it like it's Orangina. You must let it bloom on your tongue."

"Of course," I said, laughing, and somehow he thought I was laughing with him rather than at him. Then, quite rapidly, the veal arrived, a pallid piece of meat all but floating in a viscous vile sauce, and I knew consuming it would take effort. I asked how he had first met Genevieve and he paused, holding one admonitory finger in the air while chewing his veal with squirrel-fast jaws. "She was climbing her family tree." Then he laughed, roared, at his own anemic joke, showing the mercury fillings of his upper teeth. "I think she had issues, the poor thing, about finding a family tree dripping with knights and countesses. But it yielded only mill girls and the occasional clerk. The fantasies we spin about the past. They're a guilty pleasure."

"Why did she work at Mingo House? Was it just an internship?" I didn't really care for this veal or any other; I kept imagining the small fattening calf, confined to its pen and awaiting slaughter. In a way the calf's plight seemed analogous to Genevieve's, confined with her questionable father and then Zack Meecham.

"Oh, Mingo House meant the world to Genevieve. I think she fantasized about it being her family home. She wanted to be 'to the manor born' and she 'adopted' Mingo House in a way. In hopes that it might adopt her." His voice broke with an unfeigned grief. "And look what happened." He shoveled more veal through his lips, feeding his sorrow. For a slender man he had an enormous appetite, devouring his veal and requesting more bread by tapping the wire basket on the table and calling out "Signore!" He was also consuming enough wine to deplete the vintage, and, as he grew drunker, he again tried running his finger down my hand, so I had to keep my hands inaccessible, in my lap. "And, signore, more *vino!*"

"Ah, the Mingoes," Bryce sighed, as he pushed his empty plate away, almost pushing my butter knife off the table and onto the concrete cupid. "Of course Clara Mingo was a certified nutcase, with her séances and spiritual photographs. Did you know she was a friend of Mary Todd Lincoln's? Mary stayed at Mingo House and consulted Clara about contacting Honest Abe. I think Tad stayed there too. Genevieve couldn't look at a penny or a five-dollar bill without picturing Clara and Mary summoning the Great Beyond."

Then he mumbled something about "my little girl" and poured so much of the second bottle of wine into his glass that it slopped over and flooded the bread basket. He drank the whole glass in one quaff and smeared away tears from his eyes. He stood with the wobble of a minutes-old colt, mumbled something about needing a men's room, collided with a planter, and sent an empty wine bottle careening onto the pavement, where it shattered with a humiliating crash that caused the whole world to gawk—our fellow diners, the restaurant staff, the couples strolling hand-in-hand along the sidewalk. "How ghastly, how ghastly," he said.

Dmitri appeared, followed by the maitre d' and a woman I assumed was the manager. Bryce now seated himself not in his chair but on top of a concrete harlequin, where he began weeping, softly at first, and then with the wailing of professional mourners at Third World funerals.

"Sir, I must ask you to leave."

"My child, my child," Bryce wept. Defiantly, he hurled our bread basket to the ground.

The woman, the manager, repeated her request. "Sir, please, you must be on your way. You're disrupting everyone's…" Bryce fished for his wallet, found six fifty-dollar bills, forked over the money, and told me, "You will see me to my home, Mr. Winslow."

What choice did I have? He clung to me, weightless as a puppet, as I steadied him up Newbury Street, down Clarendon, and through the South End to his bow-fronted townhouse on Union Park. "I owe you so much." Actually, I owed him for my portion of our dinner, for the wine and veal Umbria I had left cooling on my plate.

We had just entered the front hall of Bryce's home when he suddenly announced, "I'm going to faint. My collar, it's too tight. I can't breathe, I'm having a panic attack."

Clearly Genevieve's murder had dealt him a serious blow. I helped unbutton his shirt and peel the jacket and shirt from his torso. His tie was secured in a Gordian knot that took me forever to dissect. He was hairless and he wore a ponderous gold crucifix on a chain around his neck, some seriously Catholic bling. His pants were stained; had he wet them or doused them with wine? Mercifully, he was able to remove them himself, until he sat in his scarlet bikini briefs on his long leather sofa. Seeing this stranger brought so low embarrassed me, and I forgot about the urge to escape. Tattooed on his left and right biceps, respectively, were a cross and a heart, rendered in crude, light ink, as if done with a fountain pen. "Will you be so kind as to bring me a hot towel? I have heated towel racks in the bathroom. It's just down the hallway. I'd be ever so grateful."

The house was filled with a combination of Bauhaus furniture and museum-quality art: a polychrome wood Buddha, Mayan jade, medieval iron prickets for holding cannon-sized candles, and what looked like a section of a choir stall—with slim figures of robed men, their mouths open in song. Switching on a button in the bathroom, I successfully heated a huge towel until it was omelet-warm. By the time I returned to the living room, Bryce was a bit more composed. He submerged his face in the towel, then pressed it against his concave chest, against the crucifix. I hoped he wasn't about to come on to me.

"My child was murdered."

"She was so full of life, Genevieve."

He hiccupped. "No, my child."

When he said it, it barely registered, I was that dumbfounded: "Genevieve was pregnant with my child. She was carrying my child. We hadn't planned it. It just happened. I was just thrilled, but Genevieve was…conflicted. She mentioned putting the baby up for adoption. She would never have aborted, of course." He draped the hot towel around his neck. "It's a child not a choice."

Genevieve had been carrying his child when she was murdered. His child had been murdered too. As I tried to absorb this information, my eyes wandered around the room and came to focus on a Madonna holding the infant Jesus, a Gothic statue of cracked stone. "I'm so sorry."

His sense of propriety—and heterosexuality?—returned, and he took a leather pillow from a corner of the sofa and deposited it in his lap so that it covered both his briefs and his chest.

"Of course I could have killed Zack Meecham. I was mad with jealousy. I mean I'm a little long in the tooth—thirty-eight—to be dating a college girl, but Genevieve liked older men. She was susceptible to father figures." He attempted to get up but couldn't summon the equilibrium. Instead, he fell back, hugged the pillow in a paternal fashion, and again began crying.

"Would you like some coffee?"

"No, water, without flavoring. Just Poland Spring water. It's in the refrigerator, by the pitcher of iced tea."

He was ordered, organized, as one would expect of a researcher. The refrigerator might have been located in an upscale

South End restaurant; it was crammed with roast beef and Cornish hens, all sorts of sauces for pasta labeled in Tupperware, bunches of white asparagus, trays of new potatoes, a plate of tarts, a bowl of mousse, a box of macaroons with its cover ajar, a pitcher of iced tea, and, yes, spring water. I found glasses for both of us in a cherry cabinet next to a window containing herbs sprouting from small ceramic pots.

"Wonderful, wonderful." Bryce drank the water and revived gradually. Then he tucked the pillow back in its customary place on the sofa. "The staff at Mingo House, do they believe the accounts about the monstrance?"

That was so far from my thoughts that I asked, "What?"

"A monstrance is a container for holding the host for adoration before communion." His pedantry and pretensions, once banished by the liquor, were reactivating.

"I know what a monstrance is."

"Did they mention the monstrance at Mingo House?"

"You mean the ecclesiastical silver some Mingo supposedly smuggled out of England? When King Charles the First was deposed?"

For the first time this evening Bryce Rossi seemed sincerely pleased.

"I thought that was just a legend."

"So do most scholars. But Genevieve was convinced that the monstrance—and the rest of the silver—existed. Exists."

Was that the subject of the school project she'd wanted to show me on the evening I'd found her murdered?

His voice grew hard as cloisonné: "You've thought of something. What is it?"

I wouldn't tell him, of course. "Genevieve was a bit of a romantic, don't you think? I mean, she had that cameo fetish. She'd hit the thrift shops and antique stores. She actually told me she'd like to live in the past. That's pretty unusual for a young person."

"So you think she was a fool whose opinions have no consequence." He was growing soberer by the minute.

"I didn't say that."

"Genevieve Courson was very much a realist. My God, I should know."

"You weren't at her funeral."

The potent insult didn't faze him in the least. "I was cowardly. Afraid. If I'd met her father, I was afraid...of what I might do." He'd realized I'd noticed the crude heart, his tattoo, and, caressing his right arm, covered it with his left hand. "*I could have strangled him.*"

That certainly was an interesting response. I would let him volunteer the details, to see if they matched Fletcher's. Of course the father was in some sort of trouble, but was he a sex offender?

"He's a pedophile, the old man. Genevieve always denied it, defended him, but he enjoyed photographing little girls in salacious positions. Some high school girl was having her photograph taken. For her yearbook. Old man Courson put his hand up her skirt. He claimed he was 'posing' her. Odious."

This was new, but it backed up Fletcher's version.

"Genevieve's mother was going to leave him. She'd had it with his...predilections. Then she got sick, she got breast cancer. She was too busy dying to get divorced."

To cooperate a bit, I responded truthfully about the royal silver rumor. "No one at Mingo House takes the monstrance story seriously. It's...a legend."

"Really?"

That comforted him somehow. "You'll excuse me, Mr. Winslow. I've been under a great strain." He rose.

I had to ask him the obvious question: "Do you have any idea who killed Genevieve?"

"None. None whatsoever."

"Does the name Fletcher Coombs mean anything to you?"

"It does not." When he had escorted me to the door and closed it, I counted one, two, three deadbolt locks that he drew. I'd neglected to pay for my dinner. That could be my excuse if I wished to contact him in the future.

Chapter Ten

There was no way I could determine whether Genevieve Courson was pregnant. The details of her murder in the media and the brief descriptions of her autopsy made no mention of a fetus or its possible father. But all of the friends in Genevieve's circle portrayed her as a young woman with a good deal more drama than the average "coed."

Was there a possibility the father of Genevieve's child could have been someone other than Bryce Rossi, perhaps even his dead "rival," Zack Meecham? The college community was in the process of disbanding for the summer. If I was going to investigate Zack's life, I had to do it soon. It was already June. So I headed "across the river" to Cambridge.

It was commencement week at Harvard, and Tercentenary Theatre was filled with hundreds of gray folding chairs and its trees hung with loudspeakers, cables, and crimson banners bearing the insignia of the university's individual schools—bewildering the squirrels doing their trapeze act amid all this new paraphernalia. Throngs of graduates carried red-sheathed diplomas as they tried to act blasé while showing their families the Yard and posing for photographs with the John Harvard statue. Some visitors were rubbing John's bullion-gold left foot for good luck.

My goal was Boylston House, with its white bell tower crowned by a cobalt-blue dome and courtyards cooled by venerable trees. This dormitory pretended to date from colonial times but was actually constructed during the Depression. Zack Meecham had lived here as a tutor, in close proximity with the students. Surely someone, feeling the wistfulness and nostalgia of the ending of his undergraduate career, would be willing to reminisce about this young scholar, killed in such an untimely manner.

Getting into Boylston House on this day of chaos and good-byes was easy. I just trailed along with the tide of families, all focused on their star graduate. I found myself in a common room not unlike such spaces at my prep school, with wallpaper murals of the Revolutionary War, saggy furniture, and a flat-screen TV. Many college-age young people were milling about, but, when asked, they proved to be siblings and cousins of students. Then I found an Indian girl from the subcontinent who confessed she was a senior, graduating and going to medical school in the fall. She knew Zack Meecham only by sight, but pointed to a trim blonde woman in a hot-pink Oxford cloth shirt, khaki pants, and espadrilles. "That's his, um, widow."

I certainly didn't expect this Ivy League Casanova would be married—and to such a prim and preppie spouse. Her clothing appeared ironed and starched, as though she never sat down and risked a wrinkle. She was holding a clipboard, helping a family negotiate a trunk down some challenging steps. "A little to the right and you'll be fine. Well, Susan, the very best of luck."

"Thanks so much, Mrs. Meecham," the slightly weepy girl managed to say.

"Mrs. Meecham?" I asked.

She turned with her eyebrows raised, her kiwifruit-green eyes aglitter.

"My name is Mark Winslow. I was a friend of a student I believe your husband mentored. From Shawmut College, Genevieve Courson."

Her tone had less warmth than a Baffin Island winter. "She had friends? How extraordinary." She had the debutante diction you might first think was British; it was that crisp and clipped.

"Well, I worked with her at Mingo House."

She simply stared, a basilisk in a pageboy haircut.

I had to spend all my capital. "I was the person who found her dead."

She had the frozen expression of a much older woman who's had too many facelifts, whose stiffened skin becomes a kind of desert, without emotion. But she was 28 at most. "All I can say is good riddance. Good riddance."

"I'm just curious about the murder—"

"Hers or my husband's? I consider Genevieve Courson responsible for my husband's death. She'd harassed him for months, with phone calls and intimidation. She'd harassed him in the most public, inopportune places, in class, on the subway, on his motorcycle. And being sweet-natured, Zack always forgave her. For what, in my mind, was unforgivable."

She stepped toward me, a bit too close. "There is no doubt, in my mind, that Genevieve Courson caused my husband's crash by her own actions. She pulled his hands off the controls—she had done it before—and killed him."

Her claim was so extraordinary that I found myself shaking my head.

"Oh, you doubt me, do you? Well, she could be charm itself. Why, when I first met her, I thought she was wonderful too."

The Indian student now returned. "Mrs. Meecham, is there a dolly we can use?"

"I'll show you."

Surely, now, I would lose her, but she told me, "Don't go away."

When she returned, she led me up a slate-floored staircase to her apartment. Scattered throughout the quarters were photographs of Zack, a bearded man with one unbroken, caterpillar of an eyebrow and a high-wattage grin: with his wife at a red-lacquered Shinto shrine, outside Westminster Abbey, in a drenched orange windbreaker while whitewater rafting. She served us tart, home-made lemonade.

"I apologize for the outburst. It's just that I can't discuss this with the students and my colleagues have heard it ad infinitum. But it still hurts. She tried to kill Zack twice, first his reputation and then physically.

"Zack tried to be a mentor to any student who needed it. And God knows Genevieve was a needy girl. She was a veritable black hole of need. Zack had a hard time saying No, and, when he did, that little parasite wouldn't take No for an answer."

"How did your husband meet Genevieve?"

"At a lecture on nineteenth-century urban planning. Here at Harvard. It was free and open to the public. I was there. Genevieve was in her Goth phase, with lots of piercings, black eye shadow, dressed in black. The Columbine look. Very prophetic, considering what happened.

"She asked a number of intelligent questions about the filling of the Back Bay, how it was transformed from a marsh into a neighborhood, the construction of various houses by speculators... We all went out for espressos afterward, Zack, me, a couple of other students. Genevieve asked for Zack's e-mail and, foolishly, he gave it to her. Big Mistake Number One.

"Then she dropped in during his office hours and invited herself to dinner here at the House. Zack gave her permission to audit a few of his lectures, in 'Post-Civil War America.' That's when she really glommed onto him.

"She was from a troubled family. Her father was a sex offender and her mother had just died of breast cancer. She had a boyfriend she'd nicknamed Nosferatu. We never saw him. She was trying to dump him."

"Do you know the boyfriend's real name?"

She shook her head. "Sorry."

"You say she tried to kill Zack twice, his reputation—"

"She implied Zack had made a pass at her, put his hand up her skirt. She was a liar, a scheming little liar. When Zack tried to shake her off, she spread lies, harassed him in person and via e-mail. 'If you don't see me, I'll tell everyone everything you've done.'

"Then, once, when he gave her a ride on his motorcycle, she tried to pull his hands off the handlebars, one day on Memorial Drive. She almost made Zack hit a truck."

"The time he died—"

"There was a party in Jamaica Plain for a historian from NYU. Zack went and Genevieve showed up. She had a way of weaseling into parties. I had a strep throat and stayed home. It was a miserable night, rainy, the roads were slick. Genevieve needed a ride home. She had an exam the next day. She and Zack were the only two sober people at the party. Zack lost control of his motorcycle on the Jamaicaway. He hit the tree and died instantly." She paused, glanced toward a photograph of her and Zack as a bride and groom outside what might have been Memorial Church at Harvard.

Then the vehemence returned to her voice: "It was her, I know it. She must have asked him for something and when he refused, she fought him, hit him, made him lose control. She should have died in that crash, not my husband."

She had discussed her suspicions with the police, but couldn't prove them. The evidence at the scene, the marks the tires had scored on the asphalt, the motorcycle wreckage, and the tree, provided no clues regarding a fight between the driver and passenger. Neither Zack nor Genevieve had been drinking, as confirmed by tests, via breathalyzer and the autopsy… This traumatized woman had been extraordinarily open in discussing her painful past, so much so that I hesitated to ask any more questions, except one: "Was Zack at all familiar with Mingo House?"

"He was involved with the Victorian Society of Boston. On a purely informal level. He'd go to their programs. I think they had a lecture at Mingo House once. On the spiritualist movement in the wake of the Civil War. All those widows desperate to contact their dead husbands." Here, finally, her voice faltered. "You'll have to excuse me, Mr. Winslow. Commencement makes for a long and emotional day."

Just talking about Genevieve Courson exhausted people. What could it have been like to know her well?

Chapter Eleven

In the wake of the murder, attendance at Mingo House tripled. People asked the same questions, again and again: "Is that the room where the murder happened?" "Was the Victorian Girl found in that chair?" "Can you stay here overnight?" We actually trained three extra docents to handle the crowds. The *Boston Globe* named Mingo House one of the region's ten best house museums; *The Early Show* did a segment on it. Nadia Gulbenkian kept hounding us all about the need to raise funds for the restoration of the roof, but Rudy kept fobbing her off, saying we needed a second opinion on the matter, and that all the architects were already out of town, summering on the Vineyard or Nantucket. Plus, the party in August, the fundraising bash, "An Evening with the Mingoes," in planning now for two years, would be a time to alert the public to our needs...

The second week of June, Rudy Schmitz telephoned just as Roberto and I were taking a post-coital shower. Rudy invited me to his home on Beacon Hill for "an informal brainstorming session. Seven sharp tomorrow evening." When I asked whether any other trustees were going to attend, he flattered me by saying, "Only the best and the brightest."

It turned out Rudy owned a townhouse on Mount Vernon Street, all mellow rose brick with black shutters, blossoming window boxes, and a granite stoop sporting its original boot scraper. I rapped the knocker, a gleaming brass crab. Rudy gave me a kiss on my mouth: "Welcome!" I could taste the nicotine that sustained him, helped him achieve his slender physique.

The interior of the house shocked me: it had been gutted like the carcass of a steer in a slaughterhouse—to yield an off-white shell composed around a spiraling modernistic iron staircase. Above the red marble fireplace was a Warhol silkscreen of a sexy young Rudy with dreamy, lavender-smudged eyes and naked shoulders. A massive saltwater aquarium contained bored-looking fish gliding among fan coral and seaweed.

"Please don't hate me. This house was a ruin when I bought it. The termites had been running rampant for years."

I had come to this meeting in a blue blazer and tie, but Rudy was the most casual I'd ever seen him, in a workingman's under-shirt and black denim shorts with lots of pockets with Velcro flaps. He was hairier than I'd expected, with wide bony feet pink with bunions. He must just have removed his shoes. He led me through a high-tech kitchen, outside, to an intimate garden where Jon Kim waited, in nothing but orange surfer's jams splashed with white, Hawaiian-style flowers. Jon laughed self-consciously.

"Jon, this is a surprise."

Jon had the muscular chest I'd imagined, so defined it might have been molded plastic.

"We've played hooky today. We went down to Horseneck Beach. The ocean was like bathwater."

This revelation made Jon laugh a little more, even less con-vincingly. He hadn't removed his wedding ring, but I couldn't help wonder if he and Rudy were conducting a little fling, knowing gay Asians often admire older men. And Jon had been recruited to the Mingo House board by Rudy Schmitz. Had he been "recruited" into Rudy's bed as well?

I took one of the canvas-backed director's chairs all marked "RUDY." Rudy had made chicken-salad sandwiches and offered me a bottle of Sam Adams summer ale. "I met Jon at the open-ing of Tank." Rudy twisted the cap from a fresh Sam Adams. "His company was scouting for a place to hold their Diversity Day party."

"What an, um, incredible place. The aquarium in Rudy's living room was *the small one* from Tank. Pretty amazing." Jon removed the toothpick from his chicken-salad sandwich and took an extra-large bite from it, perhaps to excuse him from further conversation.

Rudy was staring at Jon's chest with what could only be described as lust. "Jon is on board with me. With my feelings about Mingo House. We both believe it isn't *sustainable* as a museum."

Jon swallowed, took a deep draught of his ale, and coughed. "Unsustainable. Yeah."

"Jon, I thought you said we needed a major fundraising campaign, going after grants, that sort of thing… Wasn't that why you asked for my help to begin with, Rudy?"

"That was before we got the news about the roof." Rudy made a steeple out of his hands, joined them together in a pseudo-pious gesture. "The roof situation is seismic, Mark, seismic."

"But we've had a record number of people flocking to Mingo House. Thanks to poor Genevieve Courson. Mingo House is known…around the world. We had a TV crew from Bulgaria there last week."

Jon rippled his pectorals as he fidgeted in his chair. He focused his gaze on a bed of begonias flourishing against one of the walls delineating the garden. "That flurry of people won't last, of course. And the original records of the house suggest that it had substantial structural issues, right from the beginning. The foundation has buckled. Which wasn't alluded to in the architects' report."

I had purposely consumed as little ale as possible, since this was, purportedly, a business meeting. "It sounds like you two have written Mingo House off. Like you're ready to call in the bulldozers."

"There's no need to sound like Nadia, Mark," Rudy said. "The building can be used for other purposes. If massive renovations take place." Then Rudy rambled on, quoting great slabs of copy from the architects' report, as if savoring the details about the dire state of Mingo House, how the brownstone used in the house matched that used in Arlington Street Church, a stone quarried in New Jersey that became all the rage before it proved wretchedly unstable… "Perhaps there *is* a curse on the old place, who knows?"

Was Rudy coveting Mingo House as real estate? Had his developer's greed already converted it into a club, restaurant, or condominium? Gutted like his own house, of course.

"The collection—the furniture and artifacts—can be donated to the Museum of Fine Arts." Rudy reached out and almost touched Jon's knee in the intimate gesture of a sexual partner, then censored himself.

"Why would the MFA want the things in Mingo House? They're pretty mundane. It's their being together—the intact state of the household items after all these years—that makes it unique. Will the MFA want the soapstone sinks in the basement or Clara Mingo's sewing and cribbage board? Come on! …And you're still having the party in August.'

"Well, that's been planned for so long."

I'd rattled them both—the atmosphere had become taut—I was the serpent in Rudy Schmitz's garden. Rudy passed Jon another chicken-salad sandwich without offering me any. "I heard you went to Genevieve's funeral," he said to me.

"How did you know?"

"Nadia told me."

"Why was she there?"

"She's ubiquitous. Like ragweed… I wish I could have gone. I had an important financial meeting."

Jon Kim now directed the conversation away from anything to do with delicate matters. "You live quite nearby, Mark. Is that correct?"

"I'm just on the other side of the Public Garden."

"Do you live with a partner?"

"Yes, he's a law student."

"Mark is taken, Jon." Rudy sounded jealous.

"You're married, aren't you?" I asked Jon.

Rudy answered for him: "He's in transition."

"Speaking of which, I should be off." I consumed the last of my chicken-salad sandwich, and Jon said, "I should be off also. I'll walk out with you."

Rudy didn't object, but accompanied us as Jon fetched his beach things from the kitchen; these included, I noticed, a sage Ralph Lauren polo shirt, three sandy towels, aviator sunglasses with silver lenses, French tanning cream, and, to his chagrin, a box of Trojan condoms that had the audacity to drop onto the floor. "You're such a butterfingers," Rudy chided him, as Jon snapped up the condoms, turned and pulled on his polo shirt. Jon made the move and embraced Rudy, who responded by tousling his hair.

Outside, Jon said, "Rudy is a wonderful guy."

"You would know."

"He's such a Renaissance man." Jon tripped on an uneven brick in the sidewalk, and then walked ramrod-straight. "We're just friends."

Do "friends" bring condoms on jaunts to the beach? I forced him to fill the silence, let it hang in the air.

"My wife and I are separating. It's a long story, but she wants to relocate to Silicon Valley. She's getting a promotion."

"So were you a regular at Tank?"

"Once in a while. It wasn't my scene. Too much Ecstacy, a little too fast. I was just becoming…self-aware."

"Does Rudy have any suspicions as to why Genevieve Courson was killed at Mingo House?"

"No, I'm sure he's as baffled as the rest of us. She was a bright, promising young girl—so I've heard." At that moment, he found his fog-gray Audi, parked in front of Chill on Charles Street. I almost asked him to have a gelato and talk further. Now that he was leaving, he again became his formal, corporate self: "It was great to speak with you, Mark."

I never use the expression, but it came out anyway: "Take care."

Chapter Twelve

That evening, I was trying out some new material at a Chinese restaurant that, like so many in the area, doubled as a comedy club on certain nights. The Soong Dynasty was located just down the street from our condominium in a block that, a hundred years ago, had housed businesses selling sheet music and pianos; it was directly across from a colonial-era graveyard, a perpetual bit of Halloween abutting Boston Common. The restaurant's décor was a combination of Bali Hai and the Forbidden City: its walls were bristling with bamboo paneling, which gave way to a jungle of plastic bird-of-paradise plants and then a plaster volcano with a painted lava eruption calling to mind a project from a science fair. A wishing well collected pennies for children with asthma, and a yellow Styrofoam dragon writhed across the ceiling from the cash register all the way to the rest rooms.

Tonight, the audience seemed composed of all of the college students spending the summer in Boston. Portions of my routine were political humor focusing on the mayor and the Big Dig, the billion-dollar project to replace a crowded elevated expressway with a series of tunnels, still incomplete in the early 2000s. I worried how this would play with young people originally from Illinois or Virginia.

In the midst of this audience, it was all the more startling to spy Nadia Gulbenkian in her lilac tweed suit, sitting all alone by the entrance to the rest rooms, just below the dragon's spiky tail. She was sipping a cup of tea and smiling wanly while some

backslapping frat boys laughed over their Scorpion Bowls at
the next table. When she saw me, she waved her hand with the
authority of a traffic cop.

I had to squeeze past the college boys, who were evidently
football players, judging by their jerseys. "Hey, you almost spilled
our bowl, man. Are you the comedian? Are you funny? Because
the drinks here suck. They're like fruit punch."

"I'll do my best."

Nadia had actually aged since the last time I'd encountered
her. "I'm not really in the mood for comedy, but it's very urgent
that I speak with you. And I think you're…a potential voice of
reason about Mingo House."

The frat boys were laughing at photos one of them was
brandishing on his cell phone. "And that's *before* she got drunk,
before the concert."

"I've been out of town, in New Hampshire," Nadia said. "I
left just after the funeral."

"I saw you there."

"Oh, certainly. Genevieve was a little full of herself, but she
knew the score, if you know what I mean."

"I don't. Tell me."

"I'd like to speak with you in private. I wasn't sure where you
lived and I didn't want people to know I was contacting you. I
saw this show listed in the *Phoenix.*"

Nadia wasn't in the demographic for the formerly "alternative"
but now vaguely mainstream weekly paper. I noticed that one of
her customarily flawless scarlet fingernails had chipped. "What
I have to say is most urgent. And most confidential…" The frat
boys drowned out the rest of her sentences. I could see a pair of
breasts on the screen of the cell phone they were trading around.

The owner of the Soong Dynasty, Ray Leung, was near the
stage entrance, nodding to me. "We can talk after the show," I
told Nadia.

Ray ushered me backstage and gave me a plate of hot Buffalo
wings, which I slid onto the vanity table next to my cue cards.
I ate a couple of wings and got sauce on my shirt, of course.

The clubs had changed since my stint doing improv in the Nineties. They were smoke-free, so I didn't feel polluted at the end of a night. The complimentary food was just as unhealthy: baskets of French fries, nachos, onion rings. People ask where comedy comes from—from an aquifer of wit and the isolation of the observer, I'd say. Wit bubbles up and surprises you, spontaneous as a sneeze. And you need isolation and its silence in order to observe, ponder, and comment on your surroundings.

Checking my face in the mirror, I saw to my relief that a shaving cut near my nose had healed. Miriam and Chloe had persuaded me to try meditation, so, to calm my flickering nerves, I closed my eyes and began letting the mantra float in and out of my consciousness when Ray interrupted: "Hey, Siddhartha, I never knew you were that religious. Is your new material that bad? Sorry to bother you, but there's a friend of yours who's very agitated and says you want to talk to her. "

Nadia barged right in. "Just ignore me for now. Those college kids got on my nerves. I'll wait here until your act is over. I'm sure you'll be hilarious. I think I remember how to laugh."

"Nadia, you don't look well."

Behind her back, Ray Leung was mouthing "Want me to…?" and jabbing his finger in the direction of the door.

"You can wait here, of course, Nadia," I said as much to Ray as to Nadia. Ray shrugged as though he thought I was crazy and went off to command the stage, blaring, "Ladies and gentlemen, please welcome one of Boston's finest comics…Mark Winslow," which generated some robust applause.

The routine went fine. I did some of the Big Dig jokes in the voice of a new character, an engineer whose background was building sand castles at Revere Beach. Others were done in various voices: "Hey, when they said this was the Big Dig, who would have thought they meant digging in our pockets? Twelve billion dollars from grown men playing in the mud…"

A few people actually gave me a standing ovation, but some were on their way to the rest rooms. "You're a great audience," I said, bowing, "Thanks so much." In the area of the cash register,

I thought I recognized a familiar face, our Asian entrepreneur, but Ray Leung had a number of hunky nephews moonlighting at the place.

Then I ducked backstage to find, Sherry, Ray Leung's wife, sobbing, and Ray on his cell phone, looking like he'd never laughed in his life: "…Yes, the Soong Dynasty. It looks like she's already dead. She must have collapsed in the lavatory. I heard someone fall. Paul is giving her CPR right now…"

In the hall, one of the waiters was bending over Nadia Gulbenkian, who lay sprawled across the threshold of the door to the rest room. She's been murdered, my intuition all but shouted, and then the sirens became more shrill, audible even above the restaurant's air conditioning. I scratched at something on the wall, a gold plastic plaque of a pagoda, scratched at it to be sure this was real and not a delusion.

The EMTs, stretcher and defibrillator in hand, came in— calm and without optimism. One of them said to me, "This happened while you were in the room, sir?"

"He was performing," Ray said. "She's a friend of Mark's. She was waiting to speak with him."

"What was her name?" an EMT asked me.

"Her name is Nadia Gulbenkian."

"Did she have any illnesses? Was she taking any medications?"

They whisked her away. One minute she was present, in body at least, and the next she was gone, to what fate, I was unsure. I was convinced she would die, but no, she was to linger, comatose, in the ICU. I tried to contact the police, but they listened patiently before assuring me that no foul play was suspected in Mrs. Gulbenkian's situation.

But was Jon Kim in the audience that night? Could he have insinuated himself backstage and done something to Nadia, spiked her drink or frightened her somehow? Whoever it was in the murk, his face was as indistinct as if it had been airbrushed.

"This seems suspicious to me, her just collapsing," I said.

"You've been under a great strain, Mr. Winslow," the police told me. "What with the Courson case and all." True enough.

Chapter Thirteen

I felt I had to inform someone from Mingo House about Nadia's, what, illness, misfortune, attempted murder? So I telephoned Rudy Schmitz, the first thing in the morning, at home. It pleased me to realize that I'd woken him up. Yawning and clearing his throat, he informed me that he had to "find my contacts and drain the lizard," then, with a new outlook and an empty bladder, he was ready to listen.

"Nadia collapsed last night. Nadia Gulbenkian."

Silence.

"She's in the ICU at Boston General."

Silence, and then the sound of what might have been a refrigerator door closing and perhaps water gushing from a faucet.

So I elaborated, telling him how Nadia had happened to attend my show, seeing the ad in the *Phoenix*, but keeping secret her urgent desire to speak privately with me. "One minute she was perfectly fine, and the next, she was stretched out backstage on the floor, unconscious. It's just too much of a coincidence, Nadia in a coma so soon after Genevieve was strangled."

Now Rudy was obviously grinding coffee beans, judging by the ensuing fresh-roasted racket. "Mark, you're unduly addled. First of all, Nadia Gulbenkian was never 'perfectly fine' in her life. She's been blatantly paranoid since her husband went to Washington during the Kennedy administration and began banging as many cute young females as possible. Second, Nadia is actively delusional. Do you know she once saw a UFO hovering over a cornfield in southern Vermont? Or that she firmly believes that HIV was developed as a means of biological warfare by the CIA in a laboratory in the Gambia?" He then tortured more coffee beans, and I thought I could discern a second male voice in the background.

"And Nadia's health was marginal at best. She carries a Walgreens' worth of pharmaceuticals in that exhausted Chanel handbag—which she has a long history of abusing. She was hospitalized last June when she bungled the dosage of her Atenolol." Then he set the phone aside to remind someone: "Sweetie, you know I want my eggs soft-boiled! And don't use that carton of orange juice, it's tired."

I visualized Jon Kim, naked except for a chef's apron, cooking in Rudy's high-tech kitchen.

"I'm sorry if I'm interrupting you," I said, delving for information he had no intention of providing.

"Well, thank you for keeping me informed," Rudy said, cheerily. "We're always concerned about our Mingo House family."

Somehow the coldest people always use family analogies…

Just as I hung up, Roberto, finishing a high-calorie breakfast of French toast, sausages, hash browns, and gingko tea—to sharpen his memory and retain more of the intricacies of law—told me, "You need a vacation. How about weekend in Ogunquit?" Roberto was now collecting turn-of-the-last-century comic memorabilia, and an antique dealer had chanced upon a reasonably fresh page of a "Little Nemo in Slumberland" from 1916. "How about it? Lobster, antiquing, relaxation. Not a historic house in sight."

"I feel awful about Nadia."

"She's getting the best care possible."

"Everyone dumps on her. Just because she has a conscience."

So we embarked for the weekend, booking a room for two nights at one of the better motels along the Marginal Way. Ogunquit was a much shorter drive than Cape Cod, especially

Provincetown, and slower, more sedate, less of a scene. And Maine lacked the associations with Chloe's kidnapping and Lucas Mikkonen's fraudulent Norse commune. Since the sea water in Maine is ankle-cracking cold, even as far south as Ogunquit, we immediately swam in the motel's heated outdoor pool. That was a smart move, because it drizzled fitfully for the rest of our stay.

Finally, it was time to pick up Roberto's comic strip, at one of the barn-sized antique stores along one. Roberto was delighted with the newspaper, with ink vivid as a still stinging tattoo and an account of the Battle of the Somme. As we were about to leave, squeezing by a family scrutinizing a splintery old rocking horse, I spied a dummy wearing a pale green Victorian dress, with, yes, a bustle. I flagged down a member of the staff, a muscular woman in Madras shorts. I asked the price of the dress and was given a figure that was substantial but not highway robbery. "It's a theatrical piece from a production at the Ogunquit Playhouse," the woman said. "It's supposed to look like silk, but it's some kind of polyester. I think it was used in a run of *The Importance of Being Earnest*. We just sold it."

Thinking of some fetishist, of Genevieve's killer, I asked, "Who...?"

"This is going to a photographer in Portland. In the Old Port. So people can dress up and have an 'old-fashioned' photograph taken."

They had places like that in Rockport, where you could "become" a Wild West outlaw with chaps and gun, a saloon girl with spangles and fishnet stockings. Had Genevieve been posing for a photographer when she was killed? Was that why she'd been fitted with Victorian finery?

Going home, Roberto drove, gobbling salt water taffy and keeping his foot steady on the accelerator. He was always more assertive when behind the wheel, so, just as we were passing the York Wild Animal Kingdom, he blurted out, "You've still got Genevieve Courson on the brain. Don't deny it, you have that look."

I braced myself for a reprimand, but before I could respond, he said, "That's understandable, I mean, you found her, that must have been horrible. Awful."

Rather than asking if he wanted to stop at Stonewall Kitchen and replenish our supply of chutney, I let him continue.

"That dress is the central clue, isn't it? The dress she was found in, that made her such a media sensation."

"Yeah, absolutely." I took a piece of cranberry taffy, a flavor that doesn't really work. Then I confessed: "I went to her funeral."

"No shit, Sherlock."

Had Chloe told him, was she a little tattletale? That wasn't in character at all.

"I saw you on TV. Giving Marcia Haight the bum's rush. And you were on *Good Morning America*. At least your back was, ducking into the funeral home. Hey, it's national exposure. But it isn't exactly Comedy Central, is it?" We were speeding along the Maine Turnpike, the straight highway bordered by dark conifers that hint at the vast stretches of forests up north, swaths of wilderness owned by paper companies. "Sorry. That Genevieve sounds like a piece of work, what with the perv father. That must have done a number on her head. How could it not?"

"She seemed so smart, so intelligent."

"Intelligent and messed up can go together."

Then, crossing the Piscataqua River, Roberto confided he was having second thoughts about law school. The memorization involved, the importance of precedent, was a world away from our previous lives, from the freewheeling spirit of improv. "I've been consulting the I Ching, and I keep getting this answer—"

"That can mean five different things? So it means nothing at all?"

Passing an elderly driver in a Cadillac with a "Kennebushport" bumper sticker, Roberto quoted a passage, something about birds, a fire, and a broken pot.

"That's clarity. Surely you won't change your career because of a line from the I Ching."

He was gnawing through the taffy at an alarming rate.

"Well, finding Genevieve Courson's killer would be achieving justice. You don't need the I Ching to know that."

That night, as we were unpacking, Marcia Haight broke the news of Genevieve Courson's pregnancy. "We now know that the so-called Victorian Girl, Genevieve Courson, was with child. The autopsy on the slain Shawmut College coed determined she was four months pregnant."

So Bryce Rossi, the flamboyant aesthete, was indeed telling the truth. He was the father of a child, but not by choice.

Chapter Fourteen

Rudy Schmitz called a meeting of the Mingo House board of trustees "in light of the tragedy about poor Nadia Gulbenkian," as he put it in his slightly saccharine e-mail. He scheduled the meeting at Mingo House at eight in the morning, instead of at the customary evening hour. He came bearing gifts, éclairs, Neapolitans, and biscotti from a bakery in the North End. Jon Kim was helping him serve—using the raspberry-pink, gilt-edged Mingo family china.

"Aren't these, well, museum pieces?" Sam Ahearn wondered.

Rudy ignored him. "There's a superb pastry shop in Portofino that I love, but this bakery on Hanover Street is a close second." When Rudy had said the word "love," he had gazed pointedly at Jon Kim, whose custom-tailored suits seemed to be getting tighter and sexier.

"How is poor Nadia?" Sam Ahearn asked Rudy.

"She's holding her own." Rudy bit into an éclair and consumed a draught of coffee from one of the brittle teacups. "She seems to be in stable but critical condition. So we can only pray."

I almost asked Rudy how to spell that last verb.

"It could go either way." Jon Kim opened his Darth Vader-black laptop. "I spoke to my cousin. He's a neurosurgeon in New York. He said she could remain comatose for…weeks."

Sam Ahearn, his bald pate glowing, was scorning the coffee and pastries. "Nadia is so passionate about this place, about everything. Do you know she was instrumental in moving that lighthouse down in Brewster, when it was threatened by erosion? She used her connections at *National Geographic* to get them to do an article about it, and then she helped raise funds to move the thing. And she was pressuring the Turkish government to acknowledge the Armenian genocide—"

"Yes, yes, we all have our Nadia stories." Rudy crumpled the paper doily that had escorted the éclair to his plate. "She is greatly missed. There is only one Nadia. But it is our duty to carry on as thoroughly and enthusiastically as she would have."

"Are we bound to elect an interim trustee?" Sam Ahearn asked.

"We are not," Rudy stated. "We are, however, certainly in a kind of limbo when it comes to the future of Mingo House. Unsure, literally, about the roof over our heads, and of the funds to sustain us. I think this is a time to take stock. To do an accounting of what we have in our collection." He seemed to nod toward the alleged Millet of the peasants in their wooden shoes in the autumnal field. "We need our collection appraised, from top to bottom. We need to close up shop, temporarily, and sort through our treasures."

"For what purpose?" asked Sam Ahearn.

"Simply to know where we stand."

"Are you proposing bringing Sotheby's in?" Sam asked Rudy.

"Absolutely not. Nothing as definitive or expensive as that. We can use a fellow we've worked with in the past. He's very qualified but a lot less brutal on the wallet. Bryce Rossi."

I could now ask a question I'd been pondering: "Who is this guy?"

"Bryce Rossi, Ph.D., is a superb collector who specializes in Italian art. He's an expert on the nineteenth-century painters of classical subjects that Corinth One collected. He's worked with museums in Philadelphia, Baltimore, and Denver. He's erudite, charming, and reasonably priced."

And up to his neck in Genevieve Courson's life, and, possibly, her death, I almost blurted.

"You're not proposing we sell anything from the Mingo House collection?" Sam Ahearn tilted forward, as if about to rise from his metal chair and physically challenge Rudy. "Because I can't imagine Nadia permitting something like that. Nor would I."

"We are simply taking stock." Rudy closed an empty pastry box and began winding the broken bakery string around his slender fingers, making a web or cat's cradle.

Jon Kim, tapping away on his laptop, told the group, "Getting an estimate, an appraisal, of what we have in the collection could help us, should we wish to apply for a loan or make more informed decisions in the future." When Jon stroked his hair, which he was letting grow longer, I noticed that he had jettisoned his wedding ring. Perhaps he had been boiling Rudy's egg—and then some—when I'd called.

"How would the police feel about this?" When I asked the question, both Rudy and Jon Kim blanched, as though I'd singled them out. "I mean, this was a crime scene, a murder did occur here."

"Mark, the police swept the whole place for clues. Do you realize they even discovered a stay from one of Clara Mingo's corsets wedged behind the wainscoting in the pantry? And a planchete she used in her séances, in a coal scuttle in the basement? We immediately catalogued both. Because we want a total record of everything here... Do you know that when the National Trust restored Charleston, Vanessa Bell's house in Surrey, they even saved the cigarette ends from the fireplace? We're every bit as meticulous."

"How much will this appraisal cost?" Sam asked.

Jon Kim answered. "Bryce Rossi agreed to go through the entire house and give us a piece-by-piece estimate for five-hundred dollars."

"That's extraordinarily cheap, isn't it?" Sam said.

"We are always cognizant of the bottom line," Rudy said. "And Bryce Rossi has special feelings for Mingo House."

That I already knew. Questions swarmed through my brain about Rudy Schmitz's motives and his surprise connection to

Bryce Rossi. Rudy could have met Bryce through Genevieve, at Mingo House, when Bryce called on her to explore the thrift shops. Bryce was mourning the baby he'd supposedly fathered but was also obsessed by the Mingo legend of the royal monstrance of King Charles I. But if Rudy knew Bryce beyond the brownstone walls of Mingo House, had he known Genevieve Courson as well?

As Rudy licked the éclair frosting from his slender, nicotine-stained fingers, I wondered, could Genevieve have been strangled because she knew something that jeopardized Bryce—or Rudy? And Jon Kim was a bigger player, in all senses of the word, than I'd first gauged. Was he taking minutes on his laptop? That had been Nadia's duty.

We discussed the fundraiser in August. The invitations had already gone out. Of special interest were the moneyed people we could recruit as trustees, who'd bring their wallets, contacts, and enthusiasm to the cause. "We need fresh blood, a massive transfusion," Rudy said. "And I'm pleased to report that Dorothea Jakes has agreed to fund the restoration of Clara Mingo's harp. It will be ready in time for the party, to provide music. And I've found a young student who's a musical prodigy who will be playing it."

As the meeting began breaking up, the conversation veered off into chit-chat about the exceptionally rainy summer, the Red Sox pitching, and the discovery of mosquitoes bearing West Nile virus in Brookline. (Could Nadia be sick with West Nile virus? No, they would have diagnosed that by now.) The other trustees left for their workday worlds, but my instinct suggested I linger to thank Rudy for not betraying my confidence that Nadia had been stricken where I was performing. "Rudy, thanks for keeping mum about the particulars about Nadia. Being at the Soong Dynasty and so on."

"Certainly." Rudy was still peeved about my reluctance to subscribe to his notion that Mingo House was not sustainable.

He scurried to the kitchen, laden with china. I trailed along. Jon Kim was rinsing dishes in the sink, as, held hostage by his sudsy hands, he was forced to submit to Rudy's kissing his nape. Then Jon got aggressive, nibbling the older man's mouth with erotic hunger.

"You'll make me drop the china."

"Screw the china."

"Don't you dare. I'm the jealous type, buddy."

They knew I was watching them; it stoked their libidos. Either Jon Kim had been lying before, or their relationship had evolved from platonic to intimate since our clandestine chat on Beacon Hill. Rudy allowed his stack of china to clatter onto the counter with a racket that would have made most curators cringe.

"I think that what you're proposing makes absolute sense." I needed all of my Stanislavski training to sound sincere. "We can't go forward without knowing where we are. I'm pretty much of a novice at all of this, Rudy. I've always approached history from an academic or populist point of view." Then I dared to mention her: "Sometimes I think I know less than Genevieve."

Would he rise to the bait and comment on her? …No.

Jon Kim dried his hands on a scroll of paper towel. "It makes sense to create a database of the collection. To put it all online. I promised I'd help Rudy with the grunt work."

"Hey, count me in."

Chapter Fifteen

But who were these people, the once celebrated and now extinct Mingoes? Arms dealers and spiritualists, and perhaps regicides and thieves of royal silver. Both Genevieve Courson and Bryce Rossi had researched their stories and become ensnared in the history.

They were:

Corinth Hollis Mingo (Corinth One): (1820-1895)

Clara Whicher Mingo: (1823-1904)

Corinth Hollis Mingo II (Corinth Two): (1863-1954)

Aginesse Whicher Mingo, Alva Whicher Mingo, Araminta Whicher Mingo: (1861-1874)

They had risen fast and fallen gradually, as nouveau-riche war profiteers who had played a major role in extinguishing the Confederacy but who had never been embraced by Boston's bluebloods.

Their family papers, such as they were, were kept in Corinth One's library on the third floor of Mingo House. Corinth Two had supposedly burnt his parents' diaries and much of their correspondence, an odd gesture from one of Boston's pioneer preservationists, who had enabled his home to be reborn as a museum and had endowed it generously by the standards of his time.

When Dorothea Jakes showed me the papers, I was stunned. They were crammed into a dented, Hoover-era filing cabinet, a mass of manila folders and dog-earned envelopes, stuck here and there with scotch tape and paperclips, soiled with raspberry jam, coffee stains, and worse. "Who filed these? Genghis Khan?"

"They're in much better shape than before Genevieve got to them. Everything was all mixed together, the bills and checks and newspaper clippings. And those bugs that eat paper. Silverfish? They were having a grand time. Rudy told her to just…toss some of them." She sympathized, I could tell. "But Genevieve ignored him, I think."

The files transported me to a Boston that was at once decorous yet raw, lit by gaslight, a warren of cobblestone streets thick with carriages and begging urchins, with men with wiry mutton chop whiskers and women in jet mourning jewelry (the Civil War was still a gangrenous wound in the nation's soul). In photographs, Corinth One was a stern-looking man, with agate-bright eyes behind steel-rimmed spectacles and the beard of an Amish patriarch. He had a great, fleshy mole next to his nose and a belly that strained his elaborate vest. Clara's face was smooth and broad, with not a bit of distinction or hauteur; she could have been a mill girl or a farm wife, running a loom or coaxing a frozen pump. The doomed triplets—Aginesse, Alva, and Araminta—had been flattered by the artist who had done their posthumous portrait. They were frankly homely, with buck teeth and prominent chins. Corinth Two "broke the mold" by being tall and handsome, with a look eventually appropriated by Leyendecker for the "Arrow collar man." He was pictured by the papier-mâché boulders of photographers' studios; gloating over a bison he had shot out west; strolling aboard the pre-torpedo *Lusitania*. He was photographed with a bland-faced woman an inscription revealed was Isabella Stewart Gardner, and, in his last and only color photo, driving a friend's aqua Packard. According to his obituary, he died of chicken pox during hurricane Carol on August 31, 1954. I could imagine him expiring, ending the Mingo line, while the storm outside rinsed his windowpanes.

Most of the files contained bills, for paraffin and corn starch, washboards and spats, laxatives and brandy, but Corinth Two had also left a very brief "memoir," written in his sprawling hand, apparently when he was justifying to his lawyers why he was establishing his house-museum.

I am often asked about my memories of my family, about what it was like to grow up in the household of the patriot Corinth Hollis Mingo and the medium, Clara Whicher Mingo, in an age that seems irrevocably lost, as vanished as the songs of Minoan shepherds. The most vivid presence in this house were my sisters—Aginesse, Alva, and Araminta. Though their portrait—done by Phoebe Choate Whitman, the celebrated painter of still life and the deceased—captures their physical features, it fails utterly in conveying their personalities. Their pink, sad countenances, the lace and velvet of their dresses, the lamb doll and their prim button shoes show nothing of their energy, their spirit, their raucousness as they thundered through the house—running, shouting, their flaxen hair streaming behind them, clamoring up the stairs, sliding down the banisters, pelting each other with cake and coal, shooting marbles beneath the feet of passers-by on Beacon Street. They once constructed a small but potent bomb out of a jar, a rag, and some kerosene, which they threw beneath the horses pulling the carriage of Dr. Oliver Wendell Holmes.

In all of their exploits, Alva and Araminta followed the lead of Aginesse, except when Alva played a particularly crude trick on poor, patient Rocket, our white-and-tan mutt, by tying to his tail a sleigh bell nearly big as a baseball, terrifying the animal so thoroughly that he stayed whimpering under Father's bed for two whole days. Aginesse was apt to use me as the butt of her temper, which could be ferocious. On one occasion she struck me in the temple with a musket our ancestor, Nathan Coit Mingo, had carried at the Battle of Bunker Hill. This raised a terrible lump on my skull, enough to interest Casper Newhall, of Harvard Medical School, the great debunker of phrenologists, who commented, jokingly, that perhaps my sister had permanently altered my character.

Alva was the only one of my sisters who cared at all for reading, and I can see her now, although she has lain in her grave at Forest Hills Cemetery nearly eighty years, holding a volume of Grimm's fairy tales and biting, alternately, her lip and a black whip of licorice, lost in the world of cursed castles, glass mountains, and magical gnomes. She also enjoyed spinning her small wooden top or teasing Harry, the chimney sweep's son. Once, she plunged fully clothed into the pond the swan boats ply, ruining a new pinafore and pair of shoes. (She was yearning to explore the islet that tempts all children, located in the lagoon in the Public Garden nearest Beacon Street.)

Araminta was the sole sister who appreciated the standard passions of little girls of that day: dolls, miniature tea sets, ribbons, and the like. She cherished her stuffed lamb and the ring Father brought her from New York set with a small garnet that she said glowed like Rocket's eyes in the dark.

My mother, the link between this existence and the next, was, frankly, a somewhat remote presence. She felt the weight of the world on her frail shoulders, vis-à-vis our family's role in the recent war. She felt responsible, somehow, for every bullet fired, for every cannonball discharged, whether cast in our factories or not. Reading the casualty lists, she would crumple to the floor upon seeing the name of a friend or acquaintance, and, upon being revived, retreat to her room for hours of prayer and meditation. At these times she developed the curious habit of crying and kissing her own hands. This, she would do repeatedly, especially after the deepest tragedy that was to come our way in 1874.

Then, after the war, she began in earnest her business of being a spirit guide. Business, I say, meaning hers was a serious and solemn undertaking, done with dedication and perseverance but involving no commercial exchange whatsoever. She charged not one cent for her services but gave as would a saint or prophet. My mother was not a conventionally beautiful woman, being plain but with a high patrician forehead, but *she possessed the loveliest hands I have ever beheld. And I have met the great beauties of her day and mine: Lola Montez, Otero, Mary Pickford. Father commissioned sculptures of her hands, in whitest Cararra marble, and sculptures of my sisters' hands as well.*

My sisters regarded my mother's work with the Other World as a joke, as a kind of parlor game. "Mother is summoning," they would say, or, actually, Aginesse would say, she was ever the ringleader, with her face smudged with dirt, peppermint, or chocolate pudding. Then, after a count of three (not with numbers but with their names: "Aginesse, Alva, Araminta!"), they would shriek in unison at the top of their lungs, a shrill cry that went speeding through our house. The girls would then dissolve in laughter, rolling on the floor in virtual fits, until Polly, the maid, came scolding in desperation, or Father would tell us, half in jest, "Be quiet, girls. You'll frighten away the ghosts. Someday, because of you, we may miss our chance to meet Julius Caesar." And my sisters would convulse still further, but with their hands clamped firmly across their mouths so that their glee became a quiet and private thing.

For us, paradoxically, Father was the more kind and friendly figure in the family, feared and respected though he was in the arenas of commerce and war. He would let us tug on his beard and try on his best hats and shoes. Father liked roast beef, swimming in strong currents, the Old Testament, the classics in Latin, blizzards, lawn tennis, bread pudding, and a cologne with a bracing fragrance, supposedly once used by Napoleon. On the beach at Nahant, he would join us in hunting for gaudy pebbles, branches of driftwood, and, once, lumps of ambergris. He laughed uproariously, when, at a party for one of the austere Homans girls, Aginesse toppled the lemonade well and Alva spoilt half the cake by allowing a feral cat to lick it. Father could cut silhouettes, Valentines, dragons, and monsters from sheets of paper, teach Rocket to dance on his hind legs, juggle a cluster of India rubber balls,

and "find" a gold piece "hidden" in our ears. He told won-
derful tales about Barnabas Mingo, the first of our family to
come to these shores from Norfolk, England, in 1657.

It is said Barnabas played a role in Oliver Cromwell's
revolution, not, it should be emphasized, in the military
overthrow of the Crown, but in maintaining order in its
aftermath, and, by doing this, limiting further bloodshed. It
is said he was given certain state silver and charged with its
safekeeping for the duration of his earthly life. It was agreed
upon, even by his enemies, that he kept this pledge, this oath,
religiously.

Our lives changed forever the day my sisters' ended. It was
October 1874, one of those strange days of Indian summer
that bring bright foliage and a quasi-tropical torpor, as
though August had been resurrected in all of its melancholy
and languor. We had spent the weekend at Nahant, and
Father had enjoyed swimming at Forty Steps, among the
picturesque crags and crashing breakers. Mother abhorred the
sea, it being, she maintained, "too vast and unmanageable,
like the sin and violence of mankind." She had warned the
girls not to be reckless and frequent the chowder house at Bass
Point, which she loathed but they loved, playing pranks and
doing deviltry, stealing, in one afternoon, a bag of peanuts,
a straw monkey, three raw oysters, and a tin whistle. There,
my sisters came into contact with people from what Mother
called "the venal classes," referring not to their deprivation
of money but to their deprivation of character. There were
in the town that weekend a contingent of naval men who
caused a certain amount of undue rowdiness, quarreling with
a streetcar conductor and disturbing the peace by trampling
the topiary at the Orcutt estate.

We returned home on Sunday, having closed the Nahant
house for the winter. It was on Monday morning that Mother
received a telegram that Percival Hoskins, aged 19, had
drowned rowing on the Hudson at Tappan Zee. He was a
fine, manly, broad-shouldered fellow who excelled at skeet

shooting and mimicking bird calls. He could, invariably, summon a passenger pigeon or wren by using only his breath, teeth, and fingers.

Percival's mother was a highly strung woman, the wife of the eminent manufacturer of pianos, and a neighbor of ours in the Back Bay, so she requested Mother's services immediately, and Mother rushed to aid her. In the turmoil, our household centered on the Hoskins' grief, as, gradually, like humidity steadily and stealthily clotting the air, my sisters sickened. By Tuesday morning, my youngest sister, Araminta, felt feverish, followed by Alva, and then, Aginesse, who threw Alva's wooden top and kicked at Rocket at the suggestion that she take to bed.

Dr. Hadley Austin was summoned as the girls' temperatures crept higher and they slept more, moaning softly, their golden hair damp and disheveled on the heaped up pillows. That night, the weather changed, as cold superseded the warmth we had so welcomed. Over and over, Mother and the Hoskins kept trying to rouse Percival Hoskins' shade but he remained elusive, to the distress of everyone. Father was away on business in Montreal, occupied with some sort of contract involving a foundry or factory, and, later, delayed by the washout of the railroad bridge at Colchester.

The girls rallied Wednesday morning, then, that afternoon, began their precipitous decline. Mother and the physicians kept vigil at their bedside. I slept dreamlessly, fitfully, until I awoke when the night was rent by a shrill cry—my sisters, I first thought, shrieking to tease Mother during one of her séances. Tragically, I was half-right. It was Mother's cry when the doctors set aside their stethoscopes and told her my sisters were dead.

It was six months afterward that Mother resumed her career as a medium. Eventually, she the made the mistake of conversing with the ghost of the esteemed clergyman, Reverend Asa Lawrence Fowle. This generated an outcry that resulted in our family being ostracized in both Boston and Nahant.

As our calling card tray gathered nothing but dust, Mother brooded in her room, kissing the marble likenesses of my sisters' dead hands and kissing her own living ones. Once, she took an overdose of morphine, accidentally, Father insisted, but alarming nonetheless.

Mother never broached the Spirit World again, in either séance or conversation. When I mentioned my sisters as surely dwelling in Heaven—which I pictured as a celestial Jerusalem, of golden adobe somewhat like a Zuni pueblo—she seized a ruler and thrashed my hand until we both broke into hot and prodigious tears. "It is this house!" she cried. "Its walls contain pestilence. They are built of blood and gunpowder!"

Father spent his remaining years in the library. That winter, the house in Nahant burnt, stuck by lightning during a freakish storm. The story circulated that the fire's cause was arson, set by a groom who was paid by Mother. This is fiction, balderdash, rot.

Sometimes, on winter nights such as this, when the sleet taps its needles upon the windows and the wind howls down the chimney in the voice of a banshee cursing my very hearth, I walk through the hall to Mother's bedroom to hold those marble hands in mine—the closest I can get to my dear lost family, now melded into Heaven, Hell, or Nothingness.

In addition to Corinth Two's memoir, there was one brittle, undated clipping of a reporter's visit to Clara Mingo.

Mrs. Mingo is a short woman, with a diminutive chin and raven-black tresses done in tight, shining ringlets. She wore a simple muslin dress of half-mourning, brown, without ornamentation, and, at her neck, a cameo portrait of her late nephew, Zephyrus Mingo, killed in battle at Antietam.

Over tea and watercress sandwiches, served on her lovely pink china imported from Bavaria, she speaks without morbidity or mysticism of "the very basic service which I provide. My role is no different from that of the men who lay telegraph cables across the bed of the Atlantic. I am offering a means of communication, where, previously, none existed. This role of medium was no more chosen by me than Moses chose to torch the burning bush which burst with God's Divine Fire."

I should say immediately that there is, in the Mingo household, not the slightest evidence that the family fortune derives from armaments. No arms or references to killing are permitted in the décor. In fact, when Mr. Corinth Hollis Mingo bought a bronze cast of the celebrated work The Dying Stag, by Winterhorst, his wife requested he remove it from the premises because of its depiction of death by gunfire. The Mingoes' sole surviving child, "Corinth Two," as his parents call him, a merry little fellow with his father's flaxen hair and his mother's blue eyes, is forbidden to play with any toy even vaguely associated with war—wooden guns, lead soldiers, miniature cannons, or daggers. For Mrs. Mingo holds that the germ of violence takes hold in the imagination when a child is very young, just beginning to teethe, or even, perchance, in the womb.

Mrs. Mingo's voice is sweet, her inflection mild, even when she is at her most passionate, as when she speaks of the visions she sees in her séances and indeed in the streets of Boston. "I was walking on Boston Common, not far from the Frog Pond, one fine May morning, when, behind two boys and their governess, I saw the youngsters' sorrowful and bloodied father, his head swathed in bandages, staring at the boys, tears streaking his weary cheeks. Would that I could have told those children their father gazed fondly upon them... but the criticism flung against my calling rendered me mute."

The remainder of the article discussed Mrs. Mingo's habits of diet, her subsistence on boiled chicken and beef tea; the stained-glass she had donated to Trinity Church in Copley Square; her having met Empress Eugenie at Biarritz; and, of course, her séances with the wife and son "of the late President Lincoln." The account ended when "Mr. Corinth Mingo returned from his time playing billiards at his club and reminded his wife of a pressing engagement."

So Clara had fractured the family, by neglecting the living in favor of the dead. During those hours of table-rapping, of enticing the drowned Percival Hoskins, did she show any concern for her ailing daughters, press cool towels to their foreheads, fed them bouillon, pray—act?

And how must Corinth One have felt about this tragedy, caused by his wife's attitude toward his source of income? How must he have felt, having yanked his family from obscurity, bullet by bullet, only to have his wife shoot their reputation dead?

This surely traumatized Corinth Two. Corinth Two had shown no business acumen or urge to continue the Mingo line. (Was he sublimating his anger toward one or both parents?) He'd traveled, pursued three tepid romances—with an Austrian countess, a British suffragette, and the Spanish heiress to an anchovy-canning fortune—but he'd basically frittered away his life and much of the Mingo money. By the time the *Maine* exploded in Havana Harbor, ushering in Spanish-American War in 1898, the Mingo armaments factories had closed.

Chapter Sixteen

Mingo House closed for a day so that what Rudy Schmitz called "The Last Judgment" could take place with privacy and efficiency. Sam Ahearn, the other skeptical trustee, volunteered to be on hand, as of course did Rudy and his protégé, Jon Kim. Theoretically, we were present to help move things—highboys and armoires, bric-a-brac and Persian carpets—so we were decked out in shirts with fraying collars and jeans with threadbare knees and ripped-out pockets—although Sam retained his gold claddagh ring. Bryce, by contrast, was as elegant as ever, in a fawn linen suit with an art nouveau stickpin of an opal-winged hornet brightening his lapel.

He had won the stickpin last month on e-Bay. "I was awake until the wee hours, bidding away in my nightshirt, with a quart of Dutch fudge ice cream in my lap." An assistant accompanied him—a young, almost anorexic woman with black hair cut in a trapezoid of sorts, a necklace of clear Lucite cubes, and an MoMA tote bag bulging with glossy art books. "This is Cat Hodges. Cat, dear, you may *deposit votre petite bioliotechque* on the floor by that hideous Victorian coat-rack, mahogany, circa 1875."

That was an apt beginning to the day because Bryce disparaged almost every piece in the collection. He found hairline cracks in china, chips and fissures in marble, bad restoration— "Oh, they crucified this lacquer, crucified it." He would command Cat to hand him some art tome to date a figurine or plate. Cat kept close to his side, like a dog taught to heel. At times, they would touch their heads together as they read from a catalogue or monograph, whisper and giggle before Bryce would say, "Just as I thought," and Cat would scribble onto the pad as she recorded his comments.

They were an odd, disconcerting pair, but were they a couple? They acted as such, to the swelling irritation of Sam Ahearn, who muttered to me, "What team is he playing on, this Bryce guy? Can you tell me? He seems a little light in the loafers, like our fearless leader. Hey, Rudy converted the Korean Wonder Boy. I caught them kissing like lovebirds near the fountain in Copley Square. Right in front of all the little kids wading and swimming." Obviously, Sam knew nothing of my personal life. Bryce admired: four English chairs from the Restoration period, all cherubs and demons; a Chinese junk fashioned from one massive elephant's tusk; and a Duncan Phyfe table ("Good God, it's genuine! Whodda thunk?").

Bryce requested we break for lunch before tackling the Italian paintings, his specialty. Rudy had ordered us sushi—eel, soft-shell crab, tuna, and shrimp—prepared by the chef from Flex. Since Mingo House had no yard or garden, only a bleak expanse of concrete the stable and coal chute had once occupied, now being prepped to serve as the "courtyard" for our August fund-raiser, he proposed we sit on the front steps to eat.

"Won't that violate the shrine?" Jon Kim asked, referring to the teddy bears, Beanie Babies, and votive candles still persisting after the slaying of the "Victorian Girl."

Rudy snorted, swirling his gray pony tail. "Enough is enough, I say. These morbid people who inflict their cyber-grief on those of us who actually knew poor Genevieve ought to learn some limits." He scooped up the soggy stuffed animals, the withering flowers in supermarket cellophane, the Hallmark cards, and even a resin unicorn I thought Peggy O'Connell might have contributed—and pitched them into a green garbage bag, just as Bryce and Cat, who'd brought their own prosciutto and lettuce on baguettes, ventured outside.

"Are you taking it all?" Bryce blanched.

"Every blessed thing. Every damned thing, I should say." Rudy twisted a red wire around the neck of the bag. I couldn't help but notice his powerful hands. Had they been used on Genevieve? If so, why? He always spoke condescendingly of her. Was that personal or class bias or both?

"But it's her shrine."

Cat postponed biting her baguette, dousing it with extra balsamic vinegar instead.

"It's public support for Genevieve…" Sorrow fractured Bryce's voice.

Cat pressed her finger onto the back of Bryce's hand, the exact gesture Bryce had used with me during our dinner of veal Umbria, when we'd been ejected from the restaurant on Newbury Street.

Rudy lit some sort of foreign brown cigarette and sucked its essence into his lungs. "Sadly, we've had complaints from our neighbors. The other weekend, a homeless man spent the night asleep on the steps, cuddling a big plush panda. That had never happened before our little zoo accumulated. The steps reeked of urine afterward." Rudy clapped Bryce on the shoulder. "I've commissioned a more suitable way of remembering Genevieve: I'm having a placard created to display in the front hall of Mingo House. Right where our visitors can see it as our docents say a word about Genevieve. How special she was, how unique. It will be ready for the fundraiser in August."

Cat was separating a piece of fat from her prosciutto.

"Oh, thank you," Bryce said. "That's a superb idea. And something she would have appreciated. Remember when we all went out to Flex, when she first volunteered as a docent? And she was on one of her fad diets, an all-raw diet? And she ate that tuna that was so bloody it looked like a crime scene?" Then Bryce began crying and Cat rescued him with a tissue from her MoMA bag.

"Don't you just love history?" Rudy took the conversation on a detour away from homicide, describing his own experience in historic preservation, beginning with his childhood in Baltimore. He had grown up in the Guilford section of the city, in a gleaming-white colonial revival house that his great-grandfather had filled with cuckoo clocks, a reminder of his native village in the Black Forest. He could hear them even now, the dozens of clocks chiming all at once, and the little wooden birds bowing as they shot out from their holes. How many hiding places that place had contained: back stairs, porches, inglenooks, a gazebo, the little rock garden with the lily pond where he'd launched his plastic replica of a pirate ship. He remembered the tiles flanking a fireplace, especially one depicting a sexy, pelt-clad Hercules. "I couldn't have cared less about Venus." The family lived not far from Evergreen House, the Italianate pile built by the railroad tycoon John Work Garrett, with its theater painted by Leon Bakst and the graves of favorite horses marked by sugar-white slabs of marble. All of this stirred the pre-adolescent Rudy, and while his contemporaries were worshipping Johnny Unitas, Rudy began collecting case glass and lithographs of Lillian Russell. "You can see where I was headed." He coughed, blowing smoke all over us.

Rudy was the crown prince of the downtown store of Schmitz Brothers, with its black granite facade carved with Art Deco tulips. At Christmas, he was the first child to sit on Santa's exalted lap, and he got to press the button that animated the displays in all of the department store's windows, the button that set the "old-fashioned" plaster figures in motion so that they skated on ponds of glistening mock ice, bobbed their heads and "sang" carols, and waved repetitiously from miniature sleighs. "I was quite the little monster. I wanted what I wanted when I wanted it." He'd requested and received double the amount of presents the birthday after his tonsils were removed. "I got two motor scooters and two Robert Robots."

Rudy's father had helped save Fells Point, the nineteenth-century neighborhood of brick buildings—now townhouses, oyster bars, and fudge shops—from falling before the wrecker's ball. "Yes, preservation is in my blood." He was irritating the rest of us with his acrid smoke, especially Cat, who seemed ready to live up to her nickname and scratch his eyes out.

I saw an opening to obtain some information. "Rudy, how did you and Bryce meet?" He could out Bryce if he mentioned a gay setting.

"Boston is such a small town," Jon Kim cut in.

I hadn't asked him.

"We were members of the Victorian Society, right, Bryce?" Rudy stubbed out his cigarette and had the nerve to dispose of it in a tub of marigolds in front of the building next door.

"I believe so, Rudy. We've known each other since the flood."

Sam Ahearn had declined to accept any of the Flex sushi, opting instead for a calzone. "So I saw on the news that the docent, Genevieve Courson, was pregnant." Then Sam attacked his calzone as Bryce, Rudy, and Jon Kim all seemed to be fighting heartburn.

Cat cocked her head the way mannequins do, in that gesture that makes them look lynched, with a broken neck. "The media can be so ghoulish. Let the poor woman rest in peace. Why go publicizing her autopsy? Is her uterus national news? Hasn't she suffered enough? Being killed and put in costume by some kinky pervert?" Bryce leaned against her bony shoulder. "Oh, kitten… But the work Genevieve did here lives on."

"Could it have gotten her killed?" I was recalling the "something" she'd wanted to show me the evening I'd found her dead. "Genevieve told me that her mother brought her here. On her tenth birthday. To Mingo House and a ride on the swan boats. Genevieve couldn't decide which she liked better, Mingo House or the swan boats. Most kids that age would have picked the swan boats, no contest. She was very unusual."

"So who was the father of the baby she was carrying?" Sam Ahearn was clearly too immersed in his calzone to have noticed Bryce's grief. "Was she dating a fellow from college?"

I wondered whether Bryce would claim paternity. He said, "Genevieve was a very popular girl. Pretty. Vivacious. Intelligent."

"But careless when it came to sex. To not use protection in this day and age." Sam balled up the waxed paper from his calzone. "I would think the cops would make a beeline toward anybody she'd been dating. Killing a pregnant girl. How low can you go?"

Jon Kim clapped his hands and proposed we get back to work. Rudy deposited his second cigarette stub in the neighbor's planter. "I'll get that later."

We trudged back inside and Bryce began examining Corinth One's Italian paintings: of Romulus and Remus sucking the wolf's teats, of Tiberius in his villa above the cliffs of Capri, of Pompeiians eating sparrows cooked in honey. Squinting at each canvas with a magnifying glass, he seemed slightly more positive, cooing on occasion. "The pigments are bright. There's a little cracking, but no haphazard restoration. However, this was done rather late in Randazzo's career, past his prime, when he was having his worst bout of malaria…" Cat scribbled manically on her notepad.

Bryce could put no value on Clara's bizarre trove of Civil War photographs, the glass plates of hands, legs, and entrails. "I abhor violence. I'm stymied. And repulsed. That family, this house—it has a blackness."

At four, he flopped into the sofa in the library. "I'll have to beg off on doing the dining room today. This is far more taxing than I'd imagined. And the dining room is where they found poor Genevieve, isn't it?"

Sam Ahearn's bald spot seemed ready to emit heat. "Well, what's the tab? How much is this stuff worth?"

Bryce polished his hornet stickpin with a bit of his own saliva. "I'll have to pontificate a bit."

"What have you been doing all day? You brought those books, you brought your assistant. You mean to tell me that between the two of you, you can't come up with a ballpark figure for the whole kit and caboodle?"

Cat now bared her claws: "This isn't accounting, Mr. Ahearn. It's not like tabulating a grocery bill. We are not cashiers. We have to research a few issues and debate the finer points."

"Holy Toledo." Sam whistled with disgust.

"Thank you, one and all, for a very special day," Rudy complimented the group. Sam Ahearn failed to respond, but I managed a "You're welcome." Cat and Bryce scurried away; she wanted fresh grilled sardines at the Portuguese restaurant in Kendall Square and then a new Iranian film at the nearby cinema… Rudy stepped outside to make a call on his cell phone, so, finding I'd jammed a napkin smeared with wasabi mustard into my pocket, I trailed Jon Kim into the kitchen.

"Where's the trash?"

He was soaping his hands in the sink.

"Good idea. This place is even dustier than I'd expected."

"Jonny?" Rudy called from the front hall. "My maitre d' took care of that nastiness, so I'm free."

I opened the garbage bag containing the contents of Genevieve Courson's impromptu shrine. Before consigning my dirty napkin to the bag, I would rescue the little resin unicorn and perhaps give it to Peggy O'Connell; it would be the pretext to my questioning her further. As I sifted through the toy animals with their seams disgorging their moist stuffing, I also scanned the strangers' media-inspired messages: "Rest well, Victorian Girl" and "Shine on, Ginny" and "Always in our hearts." They were handwritten on the kind of stationery you could buy in drugstores—except one, which was typed on computer paper and consisted of some sort of quotation. Was it a line of Khalil Gibran, Rod McKuen, William Blake?

A cold ripple of fright rode my spine when I read it: "Vengeance is mine; I will repay." The famous verse from Isaiah, in14-point Arial type.

Rudy rounded the corner, nuzzling Jon Kim. "Why don't we jog along the Esplanade?" Rudy asked Jon.

"You've got to kick the tobacco habit. And did you get those cigarettes you put in the planter next door?"

"They're right here, Mr. Ecology." He tossed them into the garbage bag with the stuffed animals.

"Have you seen this?" I showed them the note. Rudy made the sound sometimes written as "Pshaw." "That's about the seventh one of those." He took the note and was about to rip it up, but I stopped him. "I've taken a whole stack of them to the police. They said we're bound to get kooks of all kinds leaving messages. Some sad, some nasty. And that shrine encouraged them. Now that they know poor Genevieve was pregnant, we'll probably get a whole slew of vicious ones."

Jon Kim was twirling Rudy's ponytail. "Time to go, big guy."

"Yes, Mark. We've got to lock up. You don't want to be here alone, with Clara Mingo and her ghosts."

Or Genevieve's ghost, I might have added. As I lingered alone in the kitchen, rinsing my hands one last time, I saw a figure in the concrete-lined space back of the house—a person in a hooded, green rubber poncho, standing there in the rain.

The person gestured, as if recognizing me. Then Rudy yelled from the dining room that he was alarming and locking the building.

Rudy punched in the security code and slammed the door. The rain was intensifying. "Well, the Esplanade is out but not the run," Jon Kim said, as he and Rudy dashed off toward Beacon Hill. I sprinted to Arlington Street, went east, and reached the alley at the rear of Mingo House.

It was empty, I thought. I was relieved.

"Here." Did I recognize the voice? It was male but disguised by a cold. He was hunched under the eaves of a garage, by a stack of old boards and, in a puddle, the flattened corpse of a pigeon. "You didn't tell anyone?" Larry Courson said.

"Aren't you under house arrest? Did you get permission—"

"What does it matter after what happened to my daughter?" The lines scoring his face, of age and grief and illness, had deepened, and his chin bore the stubble of a man in a homeless shelter. He was coughing, his nose congested. "I had to come, I had to see where it happened. If I saw *where*, maybe I could figure out *why*." He glared at Mingo House. "That place is evil, you mark my words. That was built with blood money, built with corpses. It's a charnel house."

"Well, Genevieve told me she loved Mingo House. She said her mother brought her there for her tenth birthday."

"Her mother had some peculiar ideas, God rest her soul."

He gripped my arm and I'm afraid I recoiled, recalling the charges leveled against him. His daughter's tragedy didn't lessen or excuse them.

"You've got to understand that I've lost everything: my child, my spouse, my reputation. Do you know what that's like?"

Of course I didn't, but I had lost, found, and again lost a father and half-brother, and any semblance of a normal childhood. "Did Genevieve tell you she was pregnant? Did she tell you who the father was?"

He noticed the dead pigeon in the puddle and cringed. "We always taught Genevieve to be comfortable with her body, never to be ashamed of the gifts God had bestowed. I took beautiful portraits of Carol nude, after she'd been diagnosed with breast cancer. She wanted a record of her body before the mastectomy."

His reassurances weren't making me more comfortable.

"Genevieve never mentioned any pregnancy to me. She knew I had enough on my plate."

And on his conscience, perhaps. Even though we had squeezed under the eaves of the garage, the wind blew the rain so that it pursued us like a sheriff's posse. We were getting soaked.

"Who do you think killed Genevieve?"

"I have no idea. If I did, I'd have addressed the situation."

By killing the killer? "I realize that some…photographers use period costumes as props. In places like Rockport. You know, dress up as a gunslinger or a saloon girl." Was it possible he had killed her, her own father, a photographer? No, he'd been under house arrest then.

"No serious photographer would do that." He glanced back at Mingo House. "Was she found on the first floor?"

"Yes, in the dining room in the back."

"In Victorian clothing."

I was tired, so I said it accidentally: "She looked beautiful."

"*You saw her?*" He clamped his hands around my throat.

"I found her."

"You never told me." The rain streamed down his face, as though the sky was supplying his tears.

"I didn't kill her."

"Are you the father?"

I was gay and partnered, I told him, and his fury subsided. I explained about the trustees' meeting and Genevieve saying she had something she wanted to show me.

"Some nonsense about Mingo House, no doubt."

"Did you leave any notes here? At Mingo House? Today or recently?"

"You think I have time…?"

"Someone left a note with a verse from the Bible." I dug it from my jeans. By now it had become stained with wasabi mustard. 'Vengeance is mine,' the Isaiah quote."

He pulled the front of his hood lower over his forehead. "Please don't tell anyone you saw me. Just give me half an hour to get away." Then he sprinted down the alley, splashing through the puddles, almost tripping over a cardboard box that had escaped from some dumpster, and was gone.

I waited fifteen minutes before walking to the police station. Thankful no one I knew was on duty, I gave the officer at the counter the note with the biblical rant. He confirmed that "Mr. Schmitz" had brought other messages, "Holy Roller stuff," and thanked me. When I told him I saw a man resembling Larry Courson loitering near Mingo House, the cop laughed, "Are you sure it wasn't Marcia Haight? She's been going undercover, so we hear. To crack the case." Perhaps Larry was allowed a little freedom, after all.

The rain had abated, and, when I returned to our condominium, Chloe shouted from the adjacent balcony: "Have you heard? It just came on as breaking news—the father is missing, the Victorian Girl's. What does that make him, the Victorian

Guy? The Victorian Dad? He disabled his ankle thing and flew the coop."

I had just shielded a man who was an accused pedophile, who could endanger a young girl like Chloe.

She was spreading her blue rubber yoga mat on the wet slate of her balcony to begin her afternoon meditation, something she and her mother were doing these days. "I know he's a creep, but I still feel sorry for him." Assuming the lotus position, she squeezed her eyes shut.

When I switched on our television, Larry Courson's sullen mug shot was dominating the news, even on CNN.

Chapter Seventeen

Bryce returned the next day to Mingo House. Cat Hodges came back too, weighted down with three canvas tote bags full of art books as well as more sculpture-sized jewelry, spheres of chrome and copper on her wrists and neck. She emanated Genevieve's kookiness without any warmth or humor. She assured Bryce she would be at his side as they dealt with the dining room, assessed the contents of the crime scene where Genevieve and her child had met death.

"Oh, Cat, dear, it fills me with trepidation."

"Yes, but it must be faced." Cat plopped her art books onto the rosewood rocker where Genevieve had been positioned by her killer. She appraised her reflection in a gilt-framed mirror, prodded her hair, and then began overturning the raspberry-pink china on the table. "Aren't these precious? If you like that sort of thing."

Sam Ahearn and Jon Kim were the only other trustees present, since Rudy had business commitments. Sam shook his head as Bryce balked at entering the dining room. Bryce and Cat reversed roles, Cat describing all the items while Bryce scribbled notes onto a coil pad. "Who's in charge?" Sam muttered into my ear.

"Oh, these must be the triplets who coordinated their births and deaths with such precision." Cat regarded the little girls with a skeptical expression. "The lacework is rendered beautifully, and so is the leather of their shoes, and the light on the little brass buttons… But they look sickly, don't they? 'Peaked,' as my grandmother used to say. Oh my, if I'm not mistaken, isn't that a…*monstrance* in the background?"

Bryce strode into the dining room, pushed past Sam Ahearn like he was a turnstile.

"There, in the background, on the shelf."

"It's a vase." Bryce pronounced it "vahse." He had changed color, gone damask-red. "I think you're way off, way off."

"What would a monstrance be doing in a portrait of an old WASP family? Weren't these people Episcopalian? Or Unitarian?" Sam Ahearn said.

"Exactly." Bryce laughed. "Exactly."

"That portrait of the little girls," Jon Kim said, "is that a Mary Cassatt?"

"It isn't a Mary Cassatt. It's by Phoebe Choate Whitman. Her initials are in the lower right-hand corner, by the doll, the lamb, on the floor. She was a painter who lived in Still Pond, Maine. She was particularly skilled at depicting children in posthumous portraits. This could have been done from a single photograph. In which, incidentally, the objects in the background might be much more discernable."

Bryce reasserted some control. "Cat, dear, let's attend to the task at hand. Our colleagues are taking valuable time from their places of business to be here."

Jon Kim and Sam Ahearn assisted Cat by pulling a sideboard away from a wall so Cat and Bryce could scrutinize its back. Jon Kim was intrigued by a collection of netsuke shaped like deer, rabbits, bear cubs, and turtles that had accumulated on the mantel above the fireplace. His "Auntie Kay" had collected netsuke in Hawaii.

Cat resumed her descriptions, dictating to Bryce, and dismissing the kinds of flaws he had noticed. "The condition and quality of the items in the dining room is a step above the objects in the rest of the house. That's expected, in a way, because this was their Sunday best, so to speak. Seldom used or used less frequently."

The rain abated just as we adjourned for lunch. Sam Ahearn treated us to ribs from a barbecue place, messy but tender, with delicious crusts of fat. Jon Kim consumed this fare as eagerly as he had the Flex sushi. He and Cat were discussing a Herb Ritts exhibit they both had admired. "That man with the tire certainly raised my blood pressure. Has grease ever looked so good?" Jon Kim said. Bryce was gnawing away at the ribs, but Cat had abstained in favor of her own soda crackers, Gouda cheese, and organic strawberries.

"They certainly are a weird pair," Sam Ahearn whispered to me as he threw a mortuary's worth of bones into the garbage bag we'd carted out to the front steps. "But at least Miss Toothpick isn't as critical of our collection. Unlike Mr. Hairline Crack, as I call him."

Today, Mr. Hairline Crack had selected a morbid choice for his lapel, a stickpin with an onyx skull and pink diamond eyes. He saw me staring. "From the school of Faberge." Then, he rushed by us, taking the front stairs two at a time, announcing, "Bathroom break, bathroom break. And we must all scrub off this delicious but disastrous-for-a-historic property barbecue sauce."

Of course 9/11 was still fresh on our minds. We discussed the latest terrorist threat. Was it code yellow or code orange? It changed color like fall foliage. "Where on earth is Bryce?" Cat eventually asked.

I'd track him down, I told them. He wasn't in the kitchen or in the first floor bathroom, and the Mingo bedrooms were all equally empty. So I scaled the stairs to the library. For some reason—playfulness, giddiness, just being happy because the sun was finally shining—I began tiptoeing as I approached the library.

Bryce was in the library, all right, up to something very bizarre. He was pressing his ear flush with the room's walnut paneling, tapping it, as if conversing with one of Clara Mingo's ghosts—or attempting to locate something embedded within the wall.

"Find the monstrance yet?" It was the first thing that came into my mind.

Bryce tried to counterfeit the laugh he had used over the veal Umbria, and failed miserably.

"So you think the monstrance was sealed in the wall? It must be awfully valuable to still capture your interest, even after what happened to Genevieve."

"It's a legend. Like the Seven Cities of Cibola."

"People died looking for those too, didn't they? Was Genevieve killed because of that monstrance? Because she'd hit a bull's eye in her research?"

Bryce dug deep into the Brioni pocket of his suit.

"Your period of mourning for Genevieve certainly was brief. You've already replaced her with a thinner, more fashionable model."

His thinness gave him the look of an ascetic, a monk from El Greco subsisting on bread and theology. How this skinny, effete man could cast an air of genuine menace was beyond my understanding, but cast it he did then and there.

"If you and your cohorts plan to shut this museum and auction off its contents so it can become—I don't know—some condominium or yuppie cigar bar, I'm certainly going to give you a fight. And I won't be alone."

"Folks…"

Bryce and I turned in tandem to see Jon Kim and his Liberace smile.

"Cat says it's back to work."

And then I saw, to my surprise, what Bryce had drawn from his pocket—brass knuckles, the kind Depression-era hoods carried.

◇◇◇

"So, how was the Last Judgment?" Roberto asked when I got home.

"Well, that ditzy Bryce kept hedging about specifics. He doesn't specify a value for anything. He just takes down a description and says he'll think about it. ...And he carries brass knuckles. Can you believe it?"

"From that crowd, I can believe anything." Roberto indicated our bottle of Bombay Sapphire, which I had raided for the occasional gimlet. "You're taking this pretty seriously. And you're drinking more. Mark, that place, Mingo House, has god-awful karma. You're stressing without even being aware of it."

My mother and stepfather, Subash Chaudry, no longer went to AA meetings when staying in a strange city, trusted themelves and their fortitude not to drink. Was I just beginning their odyssey? Would I be their age when I ended it?

Chapter Eighteen

The next morning, as Roberto was rustling up a breakfast of Texas toast, our telephone rang and a jumpy Sam Ahearn all but yelled, "I'm so glad I got you! Turn on the TV. To Channel Four."

When I did, I got a commercial for insect repellent, featuring a computer-generated mosquito buzzing a man grilling a steak.

"It's just…" I punched the remote… The footage rolling depicted a blanket-wrapped body being borne by police down the steps of a bow-fronted brick townhouse. The lurid lights of squad cars beat against the scene as the voice-over spoke: "…The murder victim is identified as forty-four-year-old Bryce Rossi, an art dealer and philanthropist…"

"You there?"

"Some of me." But I didn't trust the floor. It seemed unstable, the trap door beneath a condemned man on a gallows.

The inevitable neighbor, saying the inevitable, came next: "He was very quiet, but very friendly. He always gave my daughter ribbon candy at Christmas, and he was famous for his Halloween parties. He'd decorate his whole house with spider webs and jack-o-lanterns. He loved children and animals." Then she sobbed into her sleeve, and the camera cut to an anchor putting on his grimmest expression: "Rossi, however, was known to police, having worked as a fence of stolen art in the past."

Of course, he had those crude tattoos, a cross and a heart, prison graffiti, done in inmates' ink. And he'd carried brass knuckles. Another commercial came on. "How was he killed? Strangled?"

"He should be so lucky. He was bludgeoned. With a hammer. They found it at the scene. But get this, he was 'positioned,' their word, in the broadcast, under a medieval statue of the Madonna and Child. Like he was some kind of offering. How sick is that?"

"Genevieve was positioned. All set up for tea with Queen Victoria."

"And guess who found him? Our friend, Cat. I guess I had old Bryce wrong after all. He really did like the ladies."

"Does Rudy know?"

"I haven't told him."

Sam agreed to do that. I didn't want to be the bearer of bad news a second time.

Roberto was logging onto our computer. "The newspapers haven't got the story yet." His Texas toast was charring.

"They're linked, they have to be." I channel-surfed to get more coverage, but the stations were doing national news now. "Genevieve, then Bryce, the father of her child. And Bryce being found under a statue of a child, *the* Child."

Roberto ceased clicking the mouse. "How did you know that? Who fathered her child?"

"Bryce, um, told me," I admitted.

"Larry Courson just busted out. Could he have slaughtered Bryce because he thought Bryce strangled Genevieve? At least you were on good terms, so they can't suspect you."

Yeah, right. I didn't dare tell him that I'd quarreled with Bryce Rossi— and was witnessed by the duplicitous Jon Kim. Jon Kim might well tattle to the police, how he had seen Bryce drawing brass knuckles on me—only hours before his slaying. And how long would it take the media, via Cat or Rudy, to link Bryce Rossi to Mingo House and concoct a "curse" for the place?

The answer was four hours: Marcia Haight seized the angle for the noon news.

Two people intrigued by the "mythical" Mingo monstrance had been murdered. In a sinister, almost ritualistic manner. And

Nadia Gulbenkian hovered in critical condition, by means fair or foul. Were all of us connected to Mingo House in danger? And because of what and by whom? Now I was obligated to revisit the police and detail my sighting of Larry Courson, since Bryce had been slaughtered and Larry was obviously a suspect.

As I left the lobby, a police car came braking in front of our condominium and two officers disembarked. One I knew from the earlier investigation when I'd been interrogated about finding Genevieve's body. The cops questioned me, there beside the ashtrays filled with sand stamped with our condominium's pseudo-heraldic logo. I described the dinner I'd had with Bryce and related his believing Genevieve was carrying his child. The cops absorbed all this with blank expressions. I also mentioned the monstrance.

"We don't believe this is art-related," the cop I had met previously said.

"But had he done time? I heard that on the news. For selling a hot crucifix stolen in Miami. Was he dangerous? Could he have killed Genevieve Courson? Larry Courson is on the lam—"

The cop I had met earlier said, "Larry Courson has been seen in Boston this morning. He was seen by a woman who has a garden in the Fens. She caught him sleeping against a tool shed."

That was after I'd spoken to him back of Mingo House, so my meeting was old information. I spoke up anyway. "I saw someone loitering back of Mingo House the day before yesterday. It looked like Larry Courson."

Then one cop got a message on his walkie-talkie and the two jumped into their squad car and left me there by the ashtrays in a cloud of exhaust.

The day was sunny, the birds were trilling in the Public Garden. People crowded the swan boats as they circled the rippling, glassy water. Ducks came panhandling toward tourists and children. The shrubs around the George Washington statue, marshaled in the manner of warring chess pieces, had grown the fattest they would all year. The plantings of high summer were in place: flame-like scarlet flowers and brown, wide-leafed things resembling tobacco. A toddler squealed with joy as the wind animated his pinwheel so that it whirled and flashed in the sun-vivid air.

The scene reminded me of Genevieve: the woman I knew—or thought I knew—and the ten-year-old whose mother had treated her to a "voyage" on the swan boats. Genevieve had been luckless as the *Titanic*. Who could have wanted to end her life, to deny her this day and the thousands of days comprising her future?

Something pulled me toward Beacon Street, past Mingo House, with its diminishing number of bouquets, toward Genevieve's alma mater. Shawmut College should have emptied for the summer, or so I thought, but students were still assembling in front of the dormitories, including in front of Howard Hall. Peggy O'Connell was among them. Had Sam Ahearn seen her room, he would have tagged Peggy the "Unicorn Girl." She was smoking, something I hadn't thought she'd do, and drinking a frappe from a massive paper cup. She didn't seem happy to see me. Exhaling smoke, she stared toward a powder-blue Mercedes convertible as it began stopping. "Jesus, it's him," she said, stamping out her cigarette and pitching it into the mulch surrounding the magnolias.

Fletcher Coombs, a passenger in the frat-boy-laden Mercedes, leapt out—shirtless, muscular, and extroverted in a way I'd never imagined. "Hey, babe!" he laughed, and, I noticed that one of his nipples was pierced with a gossamer-thin ring of silver. "Let's *mooove*."

Had Peggy's scorn been for me or him? It was hard to tell until she spoke. "Guess who dropped by like clockwork, Fletcher? The ever-curious Mr. Winslow."

"We gotta pack." Fletcher had shaved his chest, something few straight men I'd encountered ever did. He was joining Peggy in giving me the kind of look most people reserve for late-night drunks on the subway.

One of Peggy's companions, who seemed, I now noticed, quite teary, asked Peggy, "Aren't you going to the remembrance for Professor Rossi?"

"Bryce Rossi? He was a professor here?"

"Well, a lecturer. He spoke a few times every year, in a Biblical archaeology class. About authenticating the Shroud of Turin and the search for Noah's ark, you know. He collected religious relics. He had a cabinet full of saints' bones at his apartment. And he gave wonderful parties on Halloween." A tear trickled down the girl's cheek. "He was murdered last night. Bludgeoned. What a horrible world. To kill such a gentle soul." She was all in pink, pink cotton halter, pink denim shorts, pink sandals. She also was very buxom. Perhaps Bryce liked that. She was very talkative; *I* liked that.

"He used to have us over to his house. It was beautiful, like a museum. He had this beautiful statue of the Virgin Mary, and the news stations are saying he was found murdered in front of it. In some kind of ritual, some kind of Black Mass!" She wept.

That, I hadn't heard.

"So Mr. Investigative Reporter, have you gotten all the information you're after?" Peggy O'Connell shifted her bulky legs. Her shorts and sleeveless blouse accentuated her weight, as did the delicacy of the gold chain encircling her thick, linebacker's neck.

"Peggy thinks you're doing a story about Genevieve."

"And now Bryce."

"Well, I'm not. But it's pretty bizarre that Bryce Rossi was murdered, so brutally. After what happened to Genevieve. And I didn't know Bryce had a connection to Shawmut."

"It was tenuous."

"Tenuous like his heterosexuality." Peggy glanced at me.

"He had the hots for Genevieve." Fletcher settled onto the concrete stoop.

Fletcher's shoulders had reddened, raw with sunburn. Perhaps he had been "catching some rays" on the lawns by the river, on the Esplanade. For people stuck in the city during the summer, it substituted as a beach—where they could tan, picnic, toss Frisbees, and display their bodies, by the lapping, weedy-smelling water. Gay men cruised there, especially after dark. I fought the urge to admire Fletcher's physique. And the pierced nipple seemed so out of character. Was I noticing it because I hoped he was secretly gay?

"No straight men wear tassel loafers *and* collect saints' bones. I mean…really!" Could Peggy be dating Fletcher? He had called her "babe." Was that cruelty or camaraderie?

"Well, teaching in a college would give him access to young girls. As it had Zack Meecham," I told them.

"Bryce thought he was quite the alpha male," Fletcher said. Earlier, Bryce had denied knowing Fletcher.

"In his dreams." Peggy crumpled the frappe cup and cast it behind the magnolias.

"I'm not doing a story. I'm not a journalist and I didn't come here on purpose, I just happened to wander by. But the chairman of the board of trustees at Mingo House dismantled the memorial for Genevieve on the front steps. So I saved a little unicorn, white resin, with a collar of red sequins. I wondered if you might have put it there."

"I hate unicorns," Peggy said. "My grandmother gave me the ones in my room. She's paying my tuition here. So my *mother* insisted I bring them along." Now she smiled, enjoying the putdown. "And I never visited Mingo House. I hated that place. I never liked Genevieve working there. So after she was killed, that was the *last* place I'd go." She eyeballed Fletcher. "Unlike some people."

Fletcher deflected the subject. "Have the cops gotten Larry Courson?"

The teary girl said she was off to send flowers in the students' name to the Rossi family. The registrar would tell her their address.

"Could Larry Courson have killed Bryce Rossi?" I asked Fletcher. "If Larry believed Bryce had strangled his daughter?"

"Couldn't any father?"

Now, the frat boys from the Mercedes, a walking Abercrombie ad, enveloped us. "Fletch, dude, you want help with your move or not? Time's wastin', bro."

Fletcher waved the frat boys away. "Change of plans, guys. Gotta take care of some last-minute shit."

"Dude, you're moody lately. You on the rag?" one of them laughed.

"Yeah, that's the title of his latest flick," another said.

Flick?

Fletcher glowered and they dispersed, one belching ballistically.

He told Peggy, "Later," and, to me, said, "Come back to my old place for a minute."

His "old place" was literally that, in an apartment building just up the street, one of the last in the neighborhood still smothered with ivy; most owners had stripped the vines away because they infiltrated brick and stone, eroding them. The foyer, all junk mail, dust, and chicken-wire tile, yielded to a lobby whose darkness was relieved only by the dingy skylight four stories above us. "They're not big on housework. The Delts." So this was a fraternity. Perhaps the customary gold Greek letters had been camouflaged by the ivy.

His quarters, on the top floor at the back of the building, boasted a view of the sailboats flecking the Charles; one boat had just capsized. Cardboard boxes monopolized much of the space in the living room. When Fletcher shut the door he drew three bolts, the way Bryce Rossi had, in vain.

"I'm scared shitless."

He stepped close to me, as if to hug or hit me.

"We all are." I hadn't realized this was true until saying it then and there. Maybe that was why I was drinking. I hoped so, I hoped it wasn't some alcoholic's gene.

"I mean, it could be Larry. Who killed that Rossi character. If Larry thought he killed Genevieve."

"Is Larry Courson capable of murder? You seemed to believe he was innocent of molesting that girl."

"People freak out."

"But if Bryce killed Genevieve and Larry killed him, why would you be in danger? Or me?"

"Hey." He slapped his chest, with the washboard stomach and convex navel. "I'm just glad I'm moving." He raided the fridge, barren compared to Bryce Rossi's, with just pickles, mayonnaise, a loaf of Wonder Bread, and…. "Want some pomegranate nectar? It's full of antioxidants. Even though it looks pretty gross." It was a new thing that summer, a pomegranate-strawberry vitamin concoction.

"Are you moving because you're afraid?"

When drinking, his muscled chest rose and fell, and the ring in his nipple glinted correspondingly. "Living here just wasn't cutting it. I mean, the guys are great, incredible. But I want to make something of myself, you know? And there's too much partying here. Music blaring until two in the morning. The Delts aren't into studying. I'm on a scholarship. I can't live like Donald Trump."

"It must be hard to concentrate with all that's happened. Losing Genevieve and now Bryce Rossi murdered."

He placed his empty glass on the kitchen counter, along with a stack of unopened bills. One, from a telephone company, was emblazoned with a red stripe and the words, "Your account is past due." "Genevieve was lost…long before she died." His voice quavered, went up an octave, became a little boy's voice for a moment: "The thing with her father, him being accused, it knocked her out of kilter, you know? Genevieve used her life like it was part of her resume. To gain experience, climb the ladder. She wanted out of her old life, out of Lynn. That Zack jerk and Rossi—they were a means to an end. Rossi was a crook, a fence. Did you hear that on the news?"

So he confirmed what Zack's widow had claimed, that Genevieve had *pursued him*. Not the other way around.

"Whose baby was she carrying?"

"God only knows. It could have been anyone's. The way she acted. When her mother got sick, she just lost it. She was, like, 'Chances are, I've got the gene for breast cancer. I could be dead at forty just like her.'" He took my empty glass and set it by his on the counter. "I was, like, 'You're half your father's gene pool, your grandmother, Mrs. Torrance, she's still going strong and she's seventy-something.'"

"Her grandmother?"

"Mrs. Torrance. Her mother's mother. She lives on Cape Ann."

His eyes met mine. Was there sexual yearning there? No, but there was more intelligence than I'd given him credit for. "Are you a private investigator?" he asked softly.

"No, Fletcher, I swear I'm not. I just happened to become involved with Mingo House. Rudy Schmitz asked me to become a trustee. Because I'm a history buff."

"Rudy, that horndog." Fletcher sniggered. "You know Larry Courson…wasn't the greatest husband in the world. He used to rough up his wife, Genevieve's mom. He's a very perfectionistic guy. Exacting. It's what makes him such an awesome photographer. Getting the perfect shot at the exact right moment. But he can be difficult."

"You're saying he has a dark side."

"He and Mrs. Torrance fought like cats and dogs."

Fletcher hadn't taken down all of his decorations. On the door, partially ajar, leading to the stairs to what I assumed was the floor below, he had taped a poster from the Museum of Fine Arts, that famous Renoir of the man in the straw hat dancing with the sensuous woman in the red bonnet. Like the women of that day, she was plump by our standards.

"Mrs. Torrance lives in Rockport."

"Really? I'm from Gloucester. Where does she live?"

"Near Halibut Point."

"She's kind of crazy. She's a Communist. She used to run this leftist bookstore in Cambridge."

"Was she at Genevieve's funeral? You never mentioned her."

"Mrs. Torrance won't be in the same room with Larry Courson. If she could blame him for Mrs. Courson's breast cancer, she would." He opened the kitchen cabinet and removed a Fiesta ware mixing bowl and two Super Bowl coffee mugs.

I decided to be bold, risk alienating him: "Why do you shave your chest?"

"It's not my choice."

That was an odd answer. "Whose was it?"

"Long story." He removed more things from the kitchen cabinets: boxes of herb tea, a bottle of Omega 3 capsules, Pop Tarts, curry powder. Then, surprisingly, from a higher shelf, he retrieved six or seven copper gelatin molds.

"You've got as many molds as Bryce Rossi."

"They were just for decoration. ...What were you doing in his kitchen?"

"Escorting him home from dinner. He's gotten hammered—" I realized the awkwardness of my adjective too late. "He wanted to talk about Genevieve. He'd told me she was carrying his child. When she was murdered."

Fletcher lugged a browning spider plant and two small phallic cactuses from the windowsill to the trash. "Genevieve had bad taste in men."

"So how come you two never...?"

"We grew up together. We were like siblings."

"Always?"

"I could never have thought of her that way, it would have creeped me out. It would have felt incestuous."

"Where are you moving?"

"I'd...rather not say... This place is expensive. These guys have expensive tastes. Did you see that Mercedes Trent was driving? You've seen the heap I have." He twisted old newspapers around the mixing bowl and tucked it into a cardboard box.

"Do you think I'm dangerous?" I laughed. It was a joke, but no humor registered in his expression.

"If I can do anything to help, feel free to call me." He scribbled his cell phone number on a junk mail return envelope and gave it to me. "Please excuse me. I have tons to do."

Fletcher Coombs was odd all right, a man of few words and fewer social skills. Being with him required "having personality for two." He had lied before, telling Mr. Courson the police had suspects in mind. He now claimed his friendship with Genevieve predated their years at St. Monica's. But he had given me a new source, accidentally, apparently—Genevieve's grandmother, whose telephone number and address were available online.

Mrs. "G Torrance," as the directory called her, had no driveway, only an unpaved path winding through woods conquered by green coils of cat briar. I felt like the prince, slicing through thorns to reach Sleeping Beauty's castle. Mrs. Torrance's house was burr-brown, seventeenth-century, with small, diamond-paned windows and a sagging roof verdant with moss. Time had warped its contours as it had settled unevenly into the ground.

No bell, no knocker greeted me at the door; the house itself seemed to shun visitors. Then, from behind me, a voice asked, "What do you want?"

It was a gray-haired woman, with the austere beauty of an elder Puritan, with the cheekbones of a model and the wardrobe of Priscilla Alden, a long dress of unbleached cotton the color of moths' wings, without ornamentation of any kind. Her shoes, however, were the kind young people favor, orange work boots from an Army and Navy store. She cradled a bouquet of tiger lilies and a pair of yellow-handled garden shears. "You're not from the media, I hope."

"I'm a friend of Genevieve's."

"God, I thought they'd found me." She looked me up and down like a tailor judging the fit of a suit. "This Victorian Girl nonsense. Summing up Genevieve as though she's the Black Dahlia. It's revolting."

"I work at Mingo House. I was asked to be a trustee this spring. Before all of this happened. Genevieve of course was a docent. She was assigned to orient me. She was so enthusiastic about history. She remembered being taken to Mingo House on her tenth birthday. The same day her mother first took her on the swan boats."

Mrs. Torrance pinched a shriveled blossom from a stem of otherwise flawless lilies. "Carol had so many bad ideas." Mrs. Torrance resembled Genevieve in the intensity of her eyes and the square heft of her jaw, but her nose was less pointed, more restrained. Her skin bore few wrinkles; she must have evaded sun long before it was recommended. "You might as well come in."

The interior of the house was scrubbed and stark. The wide-boarded floors, honey-gold, tilted slightly, throwing me off-balance here and there. The low ceilings were of hand-hewn timber and ancient plaster, and the few tables and chairs had been crafted with simplicity—which was why the walls provoked such a reaction: they were red with posters from the Russian Revolution, of Bolshevik sharpshooters in red caps and jackets, of a giant skeleton swinging a bloody scythe, running through the streets of St. Petersburg…

"From my bookstore. I had a bookstore in Cambridge. In Central Square. In the days before espresso bars." She arranged the lilies in an earthenware vase with a glaze that looked wet like slip. The room lacked modern appliances—no television, radio, computer. Mrs. Torrance seemed to read my thoughts. "I don't live in a museum. I'm not held hostage by the past. Don't think I'm some sort of Luddite. I have all of my electronics in my office, upstairs… Why did you come here, Mr.….?"

"Mark Winslow."

She kept her hands clasped, wouldn't shake mine. "I'm Grace."

What she said next came as a shock.

"Grace Mingo."

It wasn't meant to shock me, I could tell; she was being matter-of-fact. But it shocked me just the same, to hear that "extinct" name applied to a living person. "Mingo, like the house?"

"It was my mother's maiden name. I sometimes use it because, well, we have a 'tradition' in our family—of marrying bad men."

I trailed her into the kitchen, which was as high-tech as Rudy's. "Why did you come here, Mr. Winslow? Out of curiosity? Out of altruism? Or are you up to something more sinister?" She poured two black coffees into matching clay mugs, and didn't offer me sugar or cream. "I suppose those are unfair questions. I can tell you something, something I always knew, that that house on Beacon Street, that mausoleum, is cursed, unclean, defiled. It was built with blood money, built on death. Corinth Mingo was a war profiteer. He was no different from the house of Krupp. Do you know the Krupps, Mr. Winslow? The German dynasty which armed Hitler and the Kaiser? That developed the famous gun, Big Bertha. They used slave labor in their factories, under the Nazis."

The coffee seared my tongue, but she drank it without flinching. "You can't equate arming our Union troops with arming the Wehrmacht."

For an instant, she glowed, seemed younger, almost pert. "I can do anything I want. I always have."

That, I believed. "But houses don't kill people. Neither do surnames. And you're using the Mingo surname by choice."

"It's the lesser of two evils. My husband Bill, was abusive. He did wonderful things with his hands. Made all of this furniture, for example. And he did terrible things with his hands. Breaking my collarbone and two ribs. And Carol married a man just like her father. Worse, actually. Bill didn't touch little girls. Genevieve—she picked the worst of all, didn't she?" She had her grand-daughter's ability to intimidate. She had a presence. "Bryce Rossi made my skin crawl."

"You knew Bryce Rossi?"

"Well, of course. Genevieve brought him here all the time. They spent the weekend once. So Bryce could pick through our family papers, our Bible and some letters my great-great grandfather wrote to his crazy cousin, Corinth Mingo, Corinth One, as they called him. Like a monarch, nauseating. Corinth returned them, when the two of them stopped speaking."

A long, pallid scar traversed her shoulder. Perhaps the result of abuse.

"You see, my branch of the family became Quakers. Cleanth warned Corinth his blood money would do him in, that it was venomous, drinking from a poisoned well. First, Zephyrus, Cornith's nephew, was killed at Antietam, shot through the heart by a bullet from the family factory. Oh, yes, they saw it was a Mingo bullet when the surgeon extracted it.

"Then, later, the triplets died. In that horrible house. And do you know why? They had recovered from their diphtheria. They just had heavy colds. They died because the maid forgot to give them their medicine. Because the maid was busy helping Clara conduct one of her séances, to atone for the deaths the Mingo armaments had caused. See? It's all connected. Karma, as the Hindus would say. Of the most atrocious kind.

"But Carol, Carol was enamored of it all. Then she got Genevieve enamored too. And look what happened. This history attracted Bryce Rossi and he ended up killing her. Strangling her, brutally. Because she refused to marry him. A silly, epicene man. So Larry, for once, did something right—and slaughtered him."

"But do you think Bryce was the father of Genevieve's child? If he was, why would he kill his own child in the womb?"

"Bryce was after that monstrance. The monstrance of King Charles the First." She raked her fingers through her long gray hair, seemingly enjoying its strength and texture.

"Isn't that a legend?"

"Does it matter? If Bryce thought it was real? He was a collector. Collectors are compulsives. He was also a con man. A hopelessly inept one, of course. So obvious. Do you know he once tried to kiss my hand in the 'continental' manner? He'd taken a bus tour through Tuscany and thought he'd become Bernard Berenson."

"Are you afraid of Larry Courson? Now that he's escaped?"

"I was afraid of him when Carol and Genevieve were alive. Afraid he'd hurt them." She came to the verge of tears. "But now…" She crossed the kitchen, and, from a hutch displaying a set of white stoneware, produced a handgun. "I've been an NRA member for, oh, twenty or more years."

I nodded.

"Mr. Winslow, I'm old. I've lived my life. And I've seen too much. Not just the deaths of my daughter and grand-daughter, but the death of civility, idealism, the sense that there could be progress, that humankind could become better and learn from error." She put the gun back in the hutch, behind a casserole dish in the shape of a roosting hen.

"May I see the papers? The Bible and the letters to Corinth Mingo?"

Not replying, she climbed upstairs. Following was intrusive, so I just waited. When she returned, her arms brimmed with a Bible with disintegrating binding and packets of correspondence bound in brittle string and dried-out elastics, some loose, some in shoe boxes. I scanned through it all at the kitchen table, with her sitting opposite, watching me. Mindful of her presence and of her gun, I found it difficult to concentrate. The Bible contained pages recording births, deaths, and marriages in almost invisible ink. The archive included no photographs, but a plethora of pressed flowers, mostly roses and daisies, and some vellum cards from several funerals, including that of Aginesse, Alva, and Araminta.

Her ancestors' handwriting was at once elegant and illegible, elongated, made of sweeping letters so broad that three or four words often filled an entire line. These were passionate people: like Queen Victoria they underlined constantly and were frequent users of exclamation points. Eventually, Mrs. Torrance began reading a biography of Beatrice and Sydney Webb, and I came to an interesting letter, dated 1875, from Corinth One to his cousin Cleanth, the Quaker ancestor of Mrs. Torrance. Someone other than the author had scrawled, "This was the LAST," across the top of the first page in pencil.

> *My Dear Cleanth,*
>
> *You have no idea how hard this letter is to write, particularly the second adjective in my greeting. I have often been forced to endure your sanctimonious, short-sighted, and, I daresay, impractical and unpatriotic commentary on the business I have founded, nurtured, and made prosper. Your bitter viewpoint on the death in battle of our late and keenly lamented nephew, Zephyrus—as pure-hearted and*

sweet-souled a boy who ever breathed—that he was killed in part because of God's "displeasure" with my trade—was offensive in the extreme. (Clara agrees with me wholeheartedly in this matter.)

Now, you write a still more callous account of why our three young daughters were taken from us—that they are the innocent sacrifice of a vengeful Creator—that they died for the same sorry reason as Zephyrus. And you imply that I know this because the portrait I had commissioned depicted one of their favorite dolls, bought during a happy month at Saratoga, a doll in the form of a cloth lamb. This, you propose, somehow references Our Savior, God's Risen Son, the LAMB of the Holy Scripture.

UTTER RUBBISH AND BLASPHEMY!!!!!

My daughters were given the most excellent care possible when they sickened last autumn, treated by the most eminent, kind, learned, and practical men of medicine this city has. Polly Hanlon, our maid, had an unfortunate past, having been abandoned by her family at a tender age and forced to live in a squalid cellar in the North End, in a room that flooded with each tide. She was, however, morally unimpeachable in her character and conduct, with no problems of drink or impropriety whatsoever, and had made a living painting china and greeting cards, and then, eventually, moved to a modest room near Beacon Hill. She then came to the attention of the ladies' aid at our church and we subsequently offered her a post.

Her activities the day of our daughters' deaths were timely and responsible, serving tea and barley water to the Hoskins family. Polly served Clara and the Hoskins on only three occasions, for intervals no greater than ten minutes per encounter. The Lord took our daughters because their frail lungs gave way after a siege of diphtheria and a fever they picked up that weekend in Nahant.

While we bear this burden and the loss of Zephyrus, we remain aware of the losses of hundreds of thousands of others *in the war CAUSED BY THE PARTISANS OF SLAVERY AND BY THE COWARDICE OF THOSE, <u>YOURSELF INCLUDED</u>, WHO REFUSED TO FIGHT!!!*

We rejoice, however, in knowing that their souls sing God's praises this very hour in a deathless Heaven where we will see them once more, as God wills it.

I request no response from you now or EVER.

Once Your Cousin,

Corinth Hollis Mingo

"Do you have any albums? Photographs?" I asked Mrs. Torrance.

"Genevieve had those."

"Where are they now?"

"Fletcher was going to get them."

"Fletcher Coombs?"

She straightened the pile of documents. "You know Fletcher?"

"He was at the funeral."

She bowed her head. "I can't help it. I have standards. I see right and wrong. But I couldn't stand to see Larry Courson. Why he beat my daughter when she was having chemotherapy. It was hard enough seeing him at Carol's… To have to see him… I would have torn him limb from limb. Or…" She smiled in the direction of the hutch.

"I wasn't sure whether Fletcher met Genevieve at St. Monica's, in school, or if the families were close, way before that."

"Oh, they'd known each other their whole lives. I never cared for Fletcher. He came from a very reactionary family. His uncle was active in the John Birch Society. His mother was very liberal, the flower power sort, believe it or not, but she changed when she married Fletcher's father. So I've heard.

"And of course I'd run a Marxist bookstore in Cambridge, so they treated me like Alger Hiss. I remember Francis, Frank, Fletcher's father, swearing Martin Luther King was a Soviet agent, and that Castro had killed Kennedy—both Kennedys—how's that for a wacko? And he had very old-fashioned ideas about women, which I'm sure influenced his son."

Before I could ask my question, she said, "But I always felt sorry for Fletcher."

"How so?"

"Well, his sisters, he has three sisters, they're older and all so smart. They went to Brown and Smith and Wellesley. And Fletcher just wasn't a student. He had ADHD or some learning disability, but he was the lone son, so Frank put all this pressure onto him. That's why Fletcher went to parochial school, even though Frank loathes Catholics. Frank hoped the discipline would help Fletcher perform."

"Did Fletcher ever date Genevieve?"

Mrs. Torrance laughed. "No, no, of course not. My granddaughter was an intelligent young woman. Ambitious, witty, unique. Why she'd dated a Harvard professor, Zack Meecham. She brought him here too. He loved this house. I told him, 'This isn't the family manse. Stop drooling. I bought this place.'

"He was fascinated by my family because we're supposedly descended from regicides. I always took that with a grain of salt. Zack wanted Genevieve to marry him, but he was already saddled with a wife, a frigid control freak. He'd told Genevieve he'd get a divorce and then he'd teach at a university in the Midwest, where Genevieve could earn her doctorate. But Genevieve got tired of him. He was too academic, too stuffy. She wanted to be an independent researcher, unaffiliated with a university."

"Did Genevieve spend much time here?"

"Of course. She lived here after she moved out of her dorm. Her roommate was kind of a party girl who'd skip classes the whole semester and then pull all-nighters before an exam and ace it. Her roommate spent all her time at fraternities."

"Fletcher was a big fraternity guy."

"Well, he always wanted to play football, but I think he was too small, so he ended up playing hockey. Until he got hit with a puck and lost some teeth."

I had finished my coffee and was easing my mug toward her, hinting for a refill, but she didn't respond. She was one of those talkers who need an audience, and anyone who'd known her grand-daughter would have sufficed. "You say Fletcher's dad had odd ideas about women. Even though he had three successful daughters?"

"I'll bet Frank opposes the Nineteenth Amendment."

"Was he ever violent? Abusive?"

"No, I wouldn't say that. He'd just pontificate, and be the consummate boor."

"Was Fletcher ever violent, physically?"

She began putting some of the family documents back into their shoeboxes. "Fletcher was never violent." One of the ancient elastics snapped. "He kept it all bottled up. I've never seen Fletcher so much as raise his voice."

"He's had no reason to. With you." I'd seen Fletcher all extroverted, seen his frat boy side, bounding from that Mercedes, hailing Peggy O'Connell—the unlikely party girl.

"Bryce Rossi—he's a different story. He collected things besides Renaissance art, did you know that? He collected what he called 'Death Row ephemera.' He bought it online—belts from an old electric chair, a pistol used to kill some Belgian prime minister, knives, *death masks*… He showed me the death mask of some cattle rustler hanged a hundred years ago in Wyoming. 'Isn't it extraordinary? You can see the pores in his skin.' He said that, and made my skin crawl."

She was warming up to the subject. How odd these Mingoes all were!

"And he had an explosive temper. He was here and he got into an argument on the telephone, about access to some papers in a library in Washington. He became maniacal, screaming. 'I have secured permission on four previous occasions. I know two members of your board. I am esteemed in the art world. Do you hear me?' Well, you could have heard him in New Hampshire! He was a vile, pretentious creature. But he was older than Genevieve, well-connected, and a mentor of sorts.

Genevieve liked older men. Having never had a decent father, ever." She brought our coffee mugs to the sink. "Would you like to see Genevieve's room? She lived here when she left her dorm at Shawmut."

"Of course."

The room, upstairs, had low sloping ceilings and a slightly slanting floor, all odd angles like the sets in German expressionist cinema, in, say *The Cabinet of Dr. Caligari*. Or *Nosferatu*. "Did Genevieve ever call Bryce Rossi Nosferatu?"

"Like the vampire film? By Murnau?"

"Yes."

She shook her head No.

The room was like a museum dedicated to Genevieve Courson, her own private Mingo House. Here were posters of paintings by George Grosz and Wassily Kandinsky; a closet of vintage clothing, including rayon Hawaiian shirts, a charcoal-gray sheath dress, and an Eighties prom gown, a mass of ruffles and flourishes. Here were beach stones, iron pyrite, and rose quartz the pink of bland watermelon; photographs of Mingo House blown up to poster-size; and one portrait of a woman I assumed was her mother, "a dead ringer" for her daughter in every sense of the world.

"Genevieve loved that photograph of Carol because it wasn't taken by Larry. I took it, on what became Carol's last birthday."

Now she offered me her hand, as a way of getting me to leave. I shook it and thanked her.

"You've told your thoughts—your suspicions—to the police," I said.

"More times than I care to recall… You won't need to contact me again, Mr. Winslow."

The Mingo send-off, twenty-first century style.

Chapter Nineteen

Grace Torrance was a strange woman, open and hostile, talkative and guarded, charming and scary. And she had convinced herself that Bryce Rossi had strangled her grand-daughter when Genevieve had sought to sever ties. Granted, I had witnessed his temper, as had she, and certainly Bryce had a fondness, even an obsession with the past, that made killing Genevieve *and* dressing her in Gilded Age finery possible, perhaps. But Bryce had ongoing business at Mingo House, his pursuit of the monstrance and his association with Rudy—why he had even gone there on business with Cat Hodges, after Genevieve's death. So why would he "contaminate" that setting by staging a homicide? If he killed, he would do it elsewhere.

But Fletcher Coombs was another story. He had a family history of misogyny and had chosen to live in the no-doubt sexist world of a fraternity. And he liked "old-fashioned" girls, as evidenced by the Renoir poster tacked to his door. But the poster could have belonged to roommates, and clearly Larry Courson valued Fletcher as a friend. A friend fit to comfort him the very day of his daughter's funeral—as his only friend, in fact, a man he physically embraced.

I wondered, was Fletcher aware that Genevieve was a Mingo through her mother's bloodline? Could he have been jealous of her position, of her "history," both personal and professional, that kept widening the gap between them?

Had he "followed" Genevieve to Shawmut, she, settling for a modest college because of financial constraints, but he matriculating because it was the best he could hope to achieve?

Trudie, the clerk at the Shawmut registrar's office, had told me Genevieve was anticipating some "money" coming way her in the future. Was Genevieve referring to her and Bryce Rossi locating the royal monstrance at Mingo House? But surely that was a long shot, and, in the unlikely event they unearthed such an artifact, it would belong to the Mingo House foundation. Unless they kept their little treasure hunt secret, and Bryce used criminal means to fence the relic into the vast art underworld of drug lords and the Russian Mafia.

—Or was Genevieve's change of fortune matrimonial: wedding a well-off man like Bryce Rossi?

The next morning, I stopped by Mingo House. "How was Martha's Vineyard?" I asked Dorothea Jakes. She was sporting a garish dress, lime-green with blue spouting whales. She must have bought it at one of the outré boutiques that push the preppie thing too far. With Dorothea was her fifteen-year-old grandson, Chris, a somewhat dim bulb whose forehead was inflamed with a persistent case of acne. I had met Chris before because his class from the Lenox School visited Mingo House on a semi-regular basis, when studying art and the Civil War.

"Well, Edgartown was great, but things have certainly gone to pot here. Rudy and Jon—I guess they're a couple—are conducting some sort of séance in the library."

In the library, Rudy and Jon Kim had moved most of the furniture abutting the wall nearest to Arlington Street: Corinth One's grandiose desk, his globe with the world a quarter pink with the British Empire, and a table supporting the model of a Spanish galleon. They had emptied the shelves on this wall of books and stacked dozens of glass plates, Clara's record of Civil War carnage, onto the damask sofa and several chairs. They were rapping their knuckles against the walnut shelves as if starting a perverse "knock, knock" joke.

"Nothing, nothing," Jon Kim kept saying. "Keep trying, it's got to be someplace," Rudy said. They were so intent that they hadn't noticed me, until Jon Kim turned to swig the can of Dr. Pepper he'd left by the copper eagle inkwell on Corinth One's desk.

"The last man who did that ended up dead," I told them.

Rudy Schmitz wheeled around.

"Bryce Rossi was doing that."

"Yes, and you were arguing with Bryce the day he was murdered. So Jonny informed me. And the docent you trained with also ended up dead." Rudy had shorn off his ponytail and was editing the gray from his remaining hair with Grecian Formula or some other such chemical.

"Gentlemen," Jon Kim said, "we must be civil."

"Do you really think that monstrance is buried in this wall?" I asked.

"Bryce Rossi did." Jon Kim set his soda directly onto the mahogany surface of the desk before catching himself and transferring it onto the green baize pad. "Bryce told Rudy—"

"Watch yourself, Jon."

"Mark needs to know." Rudy flushed red so that his complexion complemented the cartoon logo, the Leaning Tower of Pisa wearing earmuffs, on his Chill T-shirt. "Bryce told Rudy that he'd heard, through sources, that some people, art thieves, were planning a burglary here. A heist similar to the one at the Gardner Museum. To find the monstrance and sell it on the black market. Bryce had found some allusion to its whereabouts in some Mingo papers he'd chanced upon."

Was Bryce referring to the papers in Grace Torrance's house? I had found nothing relevant, but perhaps Bryce had already taken something, with or without Genevieve's knowing.

"Bryce was a fence. The media reported that. He was probably the guy planning the break-in," I said.

"Then why would he have alerted us to it, for God's sake?" Rudy, clearly addled, fetched a cigarette from his pocket, recalled his whereabouts, and then tucked it away. "Mark, I wish you would get it through your…head, I care about Mingo House, its past, present, and future. Even Nadia admits that."

"*Admits?*"

"She's regained consciousness. She spent some time in rehab and is now back at her home in Brookline. She mentioned she'd like to see you, by the way."

Jon Kim had re-mounted the small aluminum ladder they'd procured for their search and was again rapping his knuckles against the paneling.

"Why would Corinth Mingo seal this monstrance into a wall? He was a practical, no-nonsense kind of guy."

"You're forgetting Corinth had a wife," Rudy told me. "Clara Whicher Mingo was a one-of-a-kind neurasthenic, as they called them back then. Forever getting the vapors, forever taking to bed. Seeing ghosts on the stairs, in the coal shed, on the Common. Perhaps she saw the ghost of King Charles the First, with his lace collar, holding his head. Who knows? Clara could have given Corinth an ultimatum: 'Get rid of the accursed thing, or I'll leave.'"

"Hey," Jon Kim said.

"I think we're done," Rudy said.

"No, we're not. Listen." Jon Kim rapped his knuckles against the historic wood, which emitted a uniform sound of solidity until, on the uppermost shelf…

"That sounds hollow! It sounds like there's a compartment behind there," I said.

Jon Kim yanked at one particular board—"Hey, I've got something!"—then, jerkily, it slid aside as it was meant to, for the correct Mingo hand. Beyond was a cramped compartment where a square white something loomed in the murk.

"Good God!" Rudy said.

Jon Kim pulled it out—a cardboard box—was it from a department store? It was embossed with filigreed Victorian lettering and a design of bluebirds with flowers in their beaks.

When Jon Kim flipped aside the cover, we all saw, not silver, not a monstrance, but gold—a strange sort of wreath woven from—

"Hair," Rudy said. "It's a wreath made of hair."

"That's gross," Jon Kim said.

"From the triplets. Aginesse, Alva, and Araminta. The sisters who died of complications from diphtheria. The Victorians wove wreathes from their loved ones' hair. They used it in lockets and bracelets. They used it in pictures. As part of the mourning process."

"Is there anything more?" I climbed the ladder to peer into the secret compartment and saw it was empty. "No monstrance. Not here. But why hide this?"

"The Mingoes were mad," Rudy said. To put it mildly, I thought.

"But if there's one compartment, there may be others," Jon Kim said.

"See, here." Rudy pulled a yellowed strip of newsprint from beneath the wreath and showed it to Jon Kim and me.

It read:

```
Daughters of Corinth Mingo Die, Great
Tragedy Strikes Armaments Manufacturer

    The triplet daughters of Corinth Hollis
    Mingo, Aginesse, Alva, and Araminta, died of
    fever despite the valiant efforts of doctors
    and family. Mrs. Clara Mingo was reported
    prostrate with grief, insisting that the
    girls' bodies remain in their beds and pre-
    venting the undertakers from transporting
    them to the mortuary…
```

Then Rudy's cell phone began playing its ringtone of Billie Holiday's "Strange Fruit." "Yes? I thought this guy was supposed to be experienced. Are you asking *me* to come?" He clamped the phone shut. "Carnage at Flex. Our sushi chef lost the tip of his thumb while cutting up an octopus. Then he bled all over the dining area. Gotta run."

Chapter Twenty

Jon Kim insisted we go back to Rudy's townhouse on Beacon Hill. "After that treasure hunt, and all that's happened, I could use a drink. I make a killer Mojito. You game?"

It was an opportunity to sound out his opinions about the new information I'd learned lately.

He hadn't exaggerated about the cocktail. His drinks could shame those of my friend Arthur Hilliard from my old Provincetown days. Jon Kim stripped off his cranberry-red polo shirt so that he was clad in moccasins and running shorts that clung to his loins. He hadn't bothered wearing underwear or a jockstrap. In Rudy's back garden, the pink and white impatiens had risen gradually from their beds like so many bright soufflés.

"I've had a rough week, a rough summer, really. My company is facing a hostile takeover. Two other vice presidents have resigned, and, if the deal goes through, they're moving our company to North Carolina. I mean, I'm just coming out, so the last place I want to go is the Bible Belt." Jon Kim had brought us some bacon-and-scallop hors d'oeuvres left over from one of Rudy's parties but was so involved with telling his own story that he neglected to share any with me. "The upside would be I'd escape Rudy's advances." He ate the last piece of bacon. "I mean, he's a tiger in bed. He wears me out. My God, he's buff! I was shocked the first time I saw him, that he could look that good and smoke so much. But in some ways he's like a little kid, you know, got to get his way, not thinking of other people." He placed the empty hors d'oeuvres plate by his director's chair.

"I envy you, being settled and all. Settled psychologically, with your partner." He kicked off his moccasins. He and Rudy both had huge bony feet. "I'm just transitioning. Between my wife and who knows what. When I was little, in Hawaii, we lived in Kaneohe, this place near the Valley of the Temples. There's this big cemetery there, at the foot of the mountains. And this Buddhist-style temple, with a big bronze bell and a pond with carp." He burped. "It rains all the time there, this fine sprinkling mist. If you stand still, you'll grow moss. Everything mildews."

He was talking to himself as much as to me.

"I'd go to the cemetery to ruminate. To figure things out. My parents owned a hardware store, the nuts and bolts kind. They were getting divorced. My brother was off in the Marines. My sister was kind of wild, skipping school, doing ice. I was the prodigy, all A's and all alone. Pushing away the gay thing by studying twenty-four/seven, taking college-level courses at UH. But you can't study yourself out of clinical depression."

The garden was beginning to whirl. The federalist lines of Rudy's rose-red brick townhouse were warping. The Mojito was dissolving my inhibitions, and I thought of the murders: "Do you think we're in danger? Physical danger? You or me or Rudy?"

"Not me, I'm a black belt. I became one in my teens."

"Bryce was beaten with a hammer."

"He had a past. He'd probably handled some hot painting or jewel. He had some sort of conduit to the criminal world. We know that he got tipped off that a burglary might be in the works."

Jon Kim could pound down his liquor better than the late Bryce Rossi.

"Why would Rudy trust a man like Bryce?"

"Hey, I don't know Rudy's every thought. Except about sex." He grinned. "Bryce taught at a local college. The people in the various auction houses told Rudy he was competent. And Bryce was cheap and we're on a tight budget."

"No more." I shooed away his pitcher of Mojitos. Was I becoming my mother, drinking too much? Now Jon Kim had grown a third nipple. "What did you think of Genevieve Courson?"

"Well, she was a little wacky. One time she was wearing this moth-eaten mink stole, with the animals' heads and glass eyes. And she had her Goth phase, with black lipstick and pins in her ears. But she was a terrific researcher. Rudy testified to that. The paper she was writing on Mingo House was first-rate, top drawer. Rudy told me."

So Genevieve's research interested people outside Shawmut College, other than, say, Zack Meecham. "Genevieve wanted to show me something. The evening of the trustees' meeting. The evening I found her murdered."

"You're a writer and an amateur historian. She probably wanted your opinion of a paper. Maybe she had some grammatical questions."

"Had you seen any paper she'd done?"

"Uh-uh. I'm a numbers guy."

"But Rudy had? You're sure of that."

"Yup." He would reek of rum when Rudy returned later.

"Fletcher Coombs. Did you know him?"

"In the Biblical sense?"

"In any."

Jon Kim flung the ice cubes from the empty pitcher into the impatiens. "He sure is well-hung."

"Yeah, right."

"I'm serious."

"You measured it when he wasn't looking?"

"No, really, I can prove it. Cut the crap and come inside." He clasped my arm, yanked me with all of his black-belt might.

In Rudy's living room, with the Warhol and the fish tank, Jon Kim inserted a DVD into the player and the cinema-sized screen came to X-rated life. He fast-forwarded through various scenes—of giant genitals and wrestling lips.

Then, finally, he permitted the movie to run unmolested, and there, on the screen, stood a sexy young man with red hair and a shaved chest, forcing a smaller man's mouth toward his crotch. Could it be…? Next, a close-up panned from the top's six-pack, past his pierced left nipple, to his Adam's apple and, finally, lingered on his commanding, embarrassed face.

Yes, it was Fletcher Coombs.

"I'd say he's 'gay for pay,'" Jon Kim said. "He lets guys do him but doesn't reciprocate. He looks about as relaxed as a guy on a job interview. Pun intended."

"How long have you known about this?"

"Rudy bought the DVD at a shop in the South End. It was going out of business. He bought a whole slew of DVDs, including some from this local studio in Roxbury. The studio was shutting down too. Because the owner of the studio was facing morals charges. So the clerk said." Jon Kim stopped the action.

"Let me see the package. For the DVD." Fletcher wasn't on the cover of the movie, *Fresh Men Initiation*. It was produced by Zephyrus Studios on Lower Washington Street. "Did Larry Courson make this movie?" Was my head spinning because of the rum or more? Focus, focus, I told myself. "His name isn't mentioned in the credits."

"It isn't in the credits onscreen either."

"You say Rudy knew both Fletcher and Genevieve."

"I told you. He saw them at Flex. Oh—and he had them here, once, for a party. Not a sex party. It was a kind of docent appreciation day. Dorothea Jakes was here, and Nadia Gulbenkian. Rudy made Baltimore-style crab-cakes. Really delicious, with lots of horseradish. And mint juleps. His mother is from Virginia. FFV, so he says.

"We all got bombed. Even Dorothea, which was a little weird since she'd brought her grandson, Chris, as her 'date.' I played the piano, Cole Porter, badly. Genevieve kept whining that Fletcher was the world's worst dancer. But Fletcher let Rudy take liberties, grind his leg into his crotch. That's when Rudy said Fletcher confessed he'd done a skin flick."

"Was Bryce Rossi there?"

"He was never a docent."

"Why did Fletcher tell Rudy—"

"Rudy admired Fletcher's body, and Fletcher happened to blurt out that he'd done the movie. When Rudy went outside to smoke, and Fletcher went out…to get away from Genevieve, I think."

I was tipsy enough to ask him now: "Ever seen my act?"

"No, but I'm sure you're a standup guy."

Chapter Twenty-one

I took the Orange Line from Back Bay station to the appropriate stop. A few blocks away, in a neighborhood that alternated between gentrified and ominous, I located a building of pistachio-green cinderblocks that, judging by its shattered neon sign, had once functioned as a hair salon. This matched the address of Zephyrus Studios but no trace of its term in the skin trade had survived. Someone had spent extraordinary effort to cover one of its walls with the quasi-three-dimensional, cartoonists' writing that urban gangs perpetuate on flat, unguarded surfaces.

The building was bordered on its left by a lot of cornflowers and piles of sand and on its right by an old mansard-roofed house being rehabbed. A crew of workmen was prying asbestos shingles from the side of the house. Most of the crew spoke only Spanish but they found a colleague to answer my questions. "I was wondering about the building next door."

"Well, we're all wondering, buddy. Are you from the neighborhood association? That fuckin' place was supposed to be demolished back in June, but it's still here, the same goddamn eyesore."

"I was wondering..." How to phrase my question, actually. "Was this ever...Zephyrus Studios?"

"Zephyrus. What's that?"

Once prompted, I realized that I knew—it was the name of the Mingo soldier killed at the battle of Antietam, the young man referred to by the cousins, Corinth and Cleanth, in the correspondence I'd read in Rockport. Was that Larry Courson's joke about his wife's once eminent family? "There was a movie studio, I believe."

"Well, there was that beauty parlor. They sold wigs, too, and painted little designs on women's fingernails. There was a porno bookstore, if that's what you're after. But I never knew they shot movies there. It was a place with sticky floors, if you catch my drift. The neighbors got pissed off, they started a petition, then the owner got in some kinda trouble, and bang, it was shut."

"Was the owner from Lynn?"

"How should I know? The guy who owns this house here is in Europe. In It-ly for the summer. He might know. But he won't be back till mid-September."

I struck up a conversation with various people I encountered, but no one could enlighten me as to the particulars about Zephyrus Studios, let alone Larry Courson's connection to *Fresh Men Initiation*, if one existed. We were not ready for our close up, that was for sure.

Chapter Twenty-two

Nadia Gulbenkian lived in Brookline, in a cedar-shingled house, all gables and wisteria. I'd phoned ahead and been granted permission to visit her for precisely half an hour. Released from rehab the previous weekend, Nadia tired easily. But she remained the most informed, passionate, and intelligent of the Mingo House trustees.

She was attended by Henri, her nephew from Lyon who was studying at Harvard Business School. He grimaced at my box of Godiva chocolates. "You aren't aware she is diabetic. Obviously." He confiscated them, perhaps for himself. He'd thrive in corporate life, I decided.

Nadia was out back, reclining on a redwood chaise lounge, wearing a raincoat, of all things (it was a little damp), under a pergola woven through with more wisteria. She attempted to get up but merely squirmed in frustration. "See? I'm good for nothing. Nothing at all." But she'd retained her massive faux-alligator bag, and, from it, pulled out her lipstick, which she touched to her lips without consulting a mirror. Then, she unwrapped several Rollos from their tube of gilt foil, and, devouring them, said, "Mark, I just want to apologize for collapsing at your performance. I'm sure you were absolutely hilarious."

She said this without a vestige of humor or irony.

"I know there was something funny you said, and I wished I'd written it down. But then I just blacked out."

"No one slipped you anything?"

"Heavens, no!"

"Was Jon Kim there? In the audience that night?"

"Oh, no! It was a very seedy crowd."

"Everyone is so glad you're better."

"Sometime, when I'm back to normal, you must stop by and do your whole routine. Just for me."

"I'd love to."

She was sipping a can of nutrition supplement. "I'm supposed to build myself up. So they tell me. But this stuff tastes like chalk."

I just asked her outright: "Nadia, what happened to you?"

Before replying, she scanned the garden, the rain-soaked clusters of perennials: azaleas, false indigo, asters. She dropped her voice to an espionage agent's whisper, "Henri is my nephew by marriage. He's quite the mercenary vulture. I caught him taking down a Winslow Homer watercolor. Nothing attractive, some canoeist in the Adirondacks. But he was appraising it. Like that awful Bryce Rossi Rudy told me he brought in to appraise everything. A bit crass, I'd say."

"But are you all right?"

"Oh, yes. Thank God it wasn't a stroke or a heart attack. I got my pills scrambled. And I'd been nervous in that questionable crowd at the club. I'd ordered a mai tai and drank it much too fast. Those college boys got on my nerves. And those greasy chicken wings were the worst."

Other than that, Mrs. Lincoln… "But you had said you had to see me. That night."

"Absolutely." She again monitored the grounds and the back porch.

"What did you need to tell me, Nadia?"

"I remember, I'd read you'd be at the Soong Dynasty and just barged in…" She ate the rest of her Rollos. Was she really diabetic? She was desperate enough to wash them down with the nutrition supplement, which I saw was black raspberry-flavored. "It was so important. I wish I knew what it was." In her bag,

Nadia found an appointment calendar, also with a faux-alligator cover, and leafed through its pages. "No, nothing. I guess it was too important to write down."

Or remember. "Was it anything to do with who killed Genevieve? Or who killed Bryce Rossi?"

"*Oh, Lord!*" she said. Her dumbfounded expression meant she had been shielded from the media, at the rehab and here, by Henri. "Bryce Rossi was murdered?"

"I'm sorry—"

The crusty Nadia revived. "I'm not. He had a criminal past. I'd warned Genevieve about him. He was beneath her. He'd actually proposed to her. He'd gotten down on one knee—that was passé in my youth for heaven's sake. He'd taken her to the symphony so there were troops of people around. Genevieve was mortified. And he wouldn't take No for an answer. He kept badgering her. Buying her vintage clothing to buy her."

"She was pregnant. Genevieve. They found out during the autopsy."

Nadia sighed. "She never struck me as loose. How sad, the way people wreck their lives. But what happened to Rossi? Did some underworld associate do him in? And to think he had that house filled with reliquaries and crucifixes. Why, it was like visiting Philip the Second at the Escorial."

So they *had* socialized with Bryce Rossi, some of the trustees, other than Sam Ahearn.

"Bryce was killed with a hammer, in his home. His assistant, Cat Hodges, found him. It was brutal, gruesome."

"He was so attracted to the gruesome, your word, in art, all those bloody, martyred saints, do you think he…indulged in that sort of thing in his sexual life?"

"I could never read him well, read him at all, really. I mean, he kept touching me, touching my hand when we had dinner."

"*You* saw him socially?"

"Only once. I was fishing—"

"Aunt Nadia!" Henri called from the back porch. "You must not overextend yourself. Time to go, Mr. Windsor."

"Thank you so much for coming."

"Of course," I told Nadia.

As I followed Henri through the house, I felt compelled to mention my concerns for Nadia's safety. I had first thought she had been drugged, at the Soong Dynasty. "We've had a...dangerous summer around here. In connection with Mingo House."

Henri was the all-black sort: black turtleneck, jeans, sneakers, the SoHo hipster by way of the Left Bank. "Yes. The Victorian Girl. She has been of interest even in France. Did you also know this Genevieve Courson?" He gave her name a full French flourish.

"I don't think it was possible to know her. But this house is secure, right?"

"Alarmed. And I am here with my wife and sons. And my uncle, Nadia's brother, is flying in from Berkeley tonight."

"Two people associated with Mingo House have been murdered. Genevieve Courson and Bryce Rossi. Both of them knew Nadia. To some degree."

"We will take care. As you Americans say."

Framed in the front hall was a photograph of the young Gulbenkians—with Nadia resembling the lush, early Ava Gardner, and her husband—a bona-fide hunk—smiling with John F. Kennedy in the Oval Office.

"He was quite the tom cat. My late uncle. My aunt learned, how do you say it? Forbearance." He smiled for the first time. "Thank you again for the chocolate."

Chapter Twenty-three

Rudy Schmitz seemed distinctively lacking in sympathy over the death of his "friend" Bryce Rossi. "This is obviously a crime of passion," he told me on the telephone, "very much unrelated to Mingo House, thank goodness. It just demonstrates the violent world which we inhabit. I plan to light a candle in memory of poor Bryce at church this weekend." Rudy was a regular at the Church of the Advent on Beacon Hill. "Bryce tried to outrun his past but flagged, and it caught up with him.

"People laugh at the Victorians' obsession with background, but this is precisely why they required references for everything. To keep at bay the seedy and syphilitic... But Bryce dying does rather leave us in the lurch. I mean, he'd spent two full days appraising our collection, and now, this."

"Well, poor Cat must be in shock. She found him, and it was a grisly scene, according to the media."

Then Rudy muttered something to a companion about driving and "setting off" around noon. "Jonny and I are going to Crane Beach for a bit of sun. It's such a precious commodity this year. We want to take full advantage of what little is offered. I just hope the rain hasn't swollen the greenhead population."

The greenheads were large, almost carnivorous flies that left you bleeding after they bit you. They bred in the salt marshes near Crane Beach, north of Boston. "Perhaps I'll express our sympathy to Cat. From the Mingo House staff. I can discreetly inquire about Bryce's appraisals and see how much he accomplished, how much he wrote down."

Seldom had I encountered a more mercenary crew than the people associated with Mingo House. They had accountants' ink running in their veins.

Rudy had left Cat's business card at Mingo House. "Cathryn Lee Hodges, Art Historian," it read, and included a Boston number and a Back Bay address on Marlborough Street. When I called Cat, her voice was hoarse with grief, but she agreed to my coming.

She was so skinny and neat that I expected her apartment to be as clean and clutter-free as an art gallery, but it proved to be one stingy, dank room with a bricked-up fireplace and cheap Scandinavian furniture smothered with clothing: tartan coats of Scottish wool, suede skirts, some vintage things of tulle and satin...

"Wow!" I thought immediately of Genevieve.

"I'm doing a double major. In art history and fashion design."

"Really. Where?"

She mentioned an online university, then added, "I transferred from Shawmut."

"Did you know...Genevieve Courson well? She liked vintage clothing too."

"Genevieve." Cat's indigo glass beads and blue vinyl miniskirt were not exactly mourning attire. "She missed a lot of school after the accident, her motorcycle crash. And when she was around, she was very proprietary about Bryce. She acted as though she owned him. She was the same way with that Harvard professor and with poor Fletcher."

Was she packing? Was she moving, like "poor Fletcher"? And why?

"Why do you feel sorry for Fletcher? He strikes me as a person who can take care of himself."

"Fletcher is kind of a train wreck. That's what everyone assumes Genevieve was, but, from what I gather, she was a pretty tough cookie. Fletcher has trouble with women. He hasn't got the greatest social skills. He used to carry notes on dates, you know, cue cards, index cards. To help him with conversation. Genevieve said he'd done that since grammar school."

She seemed to have mastered her emotions, so I decided to ask about Bryce. "Bryce dying was such a shock."

She slammed her fist against an already bullied table. "Being made to die! It was murder. I didn't go into the living room because I could see all the blood from the foyer. And see him slumped on the floor in front of the Madonna and Child. Like he was some sort of sacrifice."

"Have you any idea—"

"Who could have killed him? Of course not. I'd have told the police and they'd have arrested him by now. But he dealt in valuable art. Someone must have taken something, some statue or coin or whatever. Do you know he had vertebrae from St. Francis of Assisi? Bryce was very religious. He was a monk for three years. At a monastery in Ohio."

"But the police said nothing was stolen. And there was no forced entry."

"Bryce was too trusting. Like a child." She began putting clothing onto hangers, some Sixties mohair sweaters in Easter egg colors.

"But Bryce and Genevieve, two people associated with Mingo House, have both been murdered in bizarre circumstances this summer. …Are you afraid?"

"I only went to Mingo House twice. The two days you were there. I'm not superstitious. I once owned a black cat and I was born on Friday the thirteenth. I'm not even religious. My mother is a Christian Scientist, but my father is a card-carrying atheist. I mean that. He's a member of this atheist society. I'm somewhere in-between."

I mentioned Genevieve Courson's pregnancy, how Bryce "I had heard" was the father.

Cat snickered. "That was one way she kept her hooks in men. Genevieve. By telling little fairy tales."

"So who was the father?"

"I have no clue. Whoever she wanted to manipulate at the moment, I suppose."

"Bryce had made some...mistakes in his life."

"Being taken in by Genevieve for instance?"

"No. Acting as a fence for stolen art. He had served time in prison. It was reported in the media."

"The media. What can you believe, even on a good day? Besides, after what I've seen, I avoid watching the news. I've seen enough, too much. You don't know what it's like to find someone dead."

"You're wrong."

She pouted and slipped two chain-link belts onto a hanger.

"I was the person who found Genevieve. At Mingo House. She was wearing this green Victorian dress, with a bustle. Something from the Eighteen-eighties. She had little lace mittens on her hands."

For an instant, a long instant, she became the freeze frame in a movie. Then her features tightened and she burst into tears. "You say that as if you relished the experience." Mouthing something I couldn't decipher, she seized a coat and flung it toward my head. I ducked and it hit the bricked-up fireplace.

"Cat—"

"Get out!"

"I only meant I understood—"

"Get out before I call the police! Maybe you found Genevieve because you put her there—after you killed her, you monster! And you never liked Bryce, all you Mingo House snobs. I saw you, sneering behind his back. You and that bald shit Ahearn!"

The appraisal was now a moot point.

Shaken, I retraced my route back home. Surely, Cat Hodges couldn't be serious about blaming me for Genevieve's murder. But she certainly was hysterical, certainly was crazy. Would she convey her crazy suspicions to the police?

I proceeded home. I almost expected a squad car idling outside of our building, but none had materialized. I wanted a gin and tonic but poured an iced tea instead and went out onto our balcony.

"Mark, you had company," Chloe Hilliard called from next door. "This man was in the lobby when I came home from school. He said he'd wait for you in the Public Garden. By the Japanese lantern his daughter liked... He was a little weird."

It could only be him. "What...did he look like?"

"Older with gray hair and a beard."

"Was he wearing a poncho?"

"It's sunny, Mark. Duh."

My only thought was to keep him away from Chloe. "Thanks... Just one of the Mingo House oddballs."

He was actually under the little granite bridge that spans the swan boats' pond. Larry Courson's facial hair differentiated him from the wanted posters, and he'd procured a preppie wardrobe Dorothea Jakes would have admired: an Oxford-cloth shirt with mint-green pinstripes and khakis held up by a cross-grain belt with a golf ball pattern. Where had he been spending his time? In homeless shelters? With loyal friends? Camped in the woods or in some alley?

"I knew I could count on you."

"You didn't touch that little girl. You are never to go near that little girl again! *Do you hear me?*"

"Don't shout, take it easy. She was just in the lobby. I asked for you, and the doorman said the girl might know where you were." Tears were accumulating in his eyes. "I thought you believed in me."

He was playing me again, the way he played everybody, using his dead daughter as a prop. "You're a pornographer, you ran Zephyrus Studios in Roxbury. Does the film *Fresh Men Initiation*, starring Fletcher Coombs, ring a bell?"

He laughed, the only time I'd ever heard him do it. "Fletcher needed some extra cash. I referred him to a friend of mine, Derek Clayton. This black guy, on the down low. Derek got into trouble when he, well, auditioned this hustler who turned out to be underage."

"Zephyrus Studios? Zephyrus isn't exactly a common name. But it's intimately connected with your wife's family—the *Mingoes.*"

"Those foul people." He averted his face while a family of tourists passed, carrying bagged souvenirs from Cheers. "It was a little joke, the name. I suggested it to Derek when he was thinking of forming his business. He wanted something classical. He was thinking of 'Hercules,' but I said, 'Derek, you've got a small-time operation. Hercules implies big.' So I suggested 'Zephyrus.' I never thought he'd use it. I mean it sounds like the name of an air freshener. Hey, I never even saw Fletcher's movies. But they helped him stay in college and buy books. His sisters all went to the Ivy League and that cost his dad big bucks."

He was a more confident, cocky man than he'd seemed previously.

"Derek wasn't very good at being a movie magnate. Well, he wasn't very good at being anything. He did a piss-poor job at whatever he tried." More tourists sidled past. "Can we walk a bit? This place is kind of busy."

"Not far. I don't want to be seen with you."

He went ahead and I followed until we met once more by the fountain at the far end of the Public Garden, the one with an angel carrying her bronze basket of grain. People seldom stop here since it's deep in shade and the fountain's basin, made of beach stones imprisoned in concrete, holds no water and no interest either for ducks or penny-pitching children.

Larry Courson said, "I know who got Genevieve pregnant. And who killed her. It was that Asian creep, Jon Kim. He was cheating on his wife."

"He's gay," I said.

"Exactly. But he didn't want to be. He even went to one of those ex-gay ministries. To get cured. While he was still with his wife and after. He went on a prayer retreat and saw a Christian psychiatrist."

The wind ruffled the trees, showering us with droplets of water from the last rainstorm. "How do you know this?"

"Genevieve told me. Jon Kim told her. When a bunch of them from Mingo House went to Rudy Schmitz's gym for sushi. Went to Flex. Jon Kim singled her out. He decided his problem was his castrating wife. He'd tried prayer and Viagra. He thought with another woman he could be quote-unquote normal."

"Did Genevieve actually say they had sex?"

"The point is he had the hots for her."

A crude phrase to use in speaking of a dead daughter. But maybe not for a pedophile.

"Genevieve didn't tell me everything." He glanced at the angel. "She had her mother's disposition, and her grandmother's. Her grandmother was a Stalinist. She admired Joseph Stalin. 'He played an honorable role in the struggle against fascism.' She said that. Honest to God."

Honesty wasn't something I associated with his family. But Genevieve had been strangled, killed using the power of someone's hands, and Jon Kim had bragged he was a black belt. Surely his hands could marshal the strength to choke the life from a college girl. "Jon Kim is a nerd, a geek. There is no way he killed Genevieve." But, saying these words, wasn't I being racist? Using the model minority Asian stereotype, long outdated by the violence of Cambodian and Vietnamese gangs.

"What about Fletcher?"

He winced. "Gimme a break. Fletcher's a wimp." He sat on the bench next to the fountain's basin. "He looks like an athlete, but all he could do was play JV hockey. Until he got hit by the puck and lost a tooth and freaked out. After that, he'd have a panic attack if he saw an ice cube." He sneered. "Fletcher is a joke."

"Did you kill Bryce Rossi? The art appraiser?"

"Of course not."

"He died just after you busted out. And he claimed he was the father of Genevieve's child."

"Did you ever meet him? I met him once when Genevieve took him to visit Carol's mother. He was a pretty unlikely Casanova."

"Bryce Rossi carried brass knuckles. He'd spent time in prison." I didn't tell him Grace Torrance's suspicions because she detested her son-in-law and I didn't care to reveal my own investigating to this man.

"For what? Stealing Girl Scout cookies?"

"Just go away. And don't go after Jon Kim." I lied: "He's traveling on business in Silicon Valley."

"Genevieve said his company was in trouble. They'd had a product recall and their CFO got the boot. Jon Kim was eating antacids by the bushel. He was really on edge."

A throng of college students approached, some sort of summer school excursion, perhaps. I was anxious at being seen with this fugitive. "Don't do anything foolish, Larry. At least you're not wanted for murder."

The students kept jostling by.

"How did you get my address?"

"Genevieve wrote it down."

Then Larry Courson merged with the stream of college students, and, once they were gone, he too had vanished.

Chapter Twenty-four

Officially, Mr. and Mrs. Jon Kim lived in a modernist high rise of glass and brick near Mount Auburn Hospital and the bird sanctuary that makes this bend of the Charles River in Cambridge off-limits to development by Harvard, the various neighboring day schools, or the upscale markets peddling wine, organic food, and antiques in the vicinity. The simplicity of the building—vaguely resembling a high school designed during the 1960s, with a lobby with concrete planters of pink-flowering African succulents—could fool you into thinking you could afford a condo here.

I'd persuaded Roberto to tag along. He was doing anything not to hit his textbooks, even sneaking out onto our balcony to babble in the voices of his old characters from our days in improv. Besides, he liked Asians; he'd once had a boyfriend, a weightlifter from Melbourne with a Mohawk and a cute Aussie accent. "Are you sure this Kim lives here? If he's separated?"

"Yes, and more importantly, his wife lives here. Rudy finally e-mailed us all a list of trustee contacts."

"And we're snooping around *why*?"

"Because Jon Kim is acting strange."

Roberto absent-mindedly kneaded the subtle pot belly his Tex-Mex cooking had sired. "Is he acting *killed-someone* strange?"

"Hard to say. Just think of this as a background check."

"What is our mission, should I choose to accept it?"

"To try to see the all-important Mrs. Kim and get a handle on Jon's darkest secrets."

"And if that fails?"

"We'll talk to whomever we can. We'll say we're interested in buying a condo. I saw a unit listed for two-million dollars with Coldwell Banker."

The lobby was locked, with no guard or concierge in sight. Someone entered the building from the Charles River side, a girl I guessed was an au pair or nanny, but she was too intent on the baby in her carriage to respond to my frenzied waving.

"I guess you're a bust with Swedish girls."

"My Norse period is definitely over."

Then a Verizon repairman exited on our side, but was too engrossed in the drama on his cell phone to stop. So we stood there, too summery dressed to seem respectable in this neighborhood, especially Roberto in his ratty Ogunquit T-shirt and cut-offs.

"How long do you have to sit before you're loitering?" I asked him. "Legally?"

"In this zip code, about ten minutes."

Soon, an ark of a limousine, big enough to accommodate a dozen giggling, prom-bound teenagers, eased quietly to the curb, and a thin woman, all rouge and frosted hair, alighted. "Alonzo," she told her driver, "bring the groceries up once you've parked the car. But not before Anastasia has had a stretch." She wore a miniskirt of sorts, and opaque white hose on her knock-kneed legs. On one wrist was a watch emphasized by an oval of diamonds, and on the other, a cuff of beaten silver. "Are you delivering something?" she asked Roberto—because he looked Hispanic?

"No. We figured you've got everything you want."

"Because, if not, we don't allow salespeople on the premises." She clutched her small bag with its clasp in the guise of a rhinestone cat's head.

"I'm a friend of Jon Kim."

When she wrinkled her brow, she aged another decade. "Are you Rudy Schmitz?" Before I could answer, she ran on like the

Boston Marathon. "Because everyone in this building, *everyone*, is on Emily's side. She has done no wrong, *she* is the wronged party. Jon knows perfectly well not to send his friends here on any little reconnaissance missions. But he wouldn't stay away, and *that's* why Emily took out that restraining order. So *he* has no business here, and *you* have no business here. *Either*."

She stamped into the lobby in her sling-back high heels. The doors to the elevator opened and she was born skyward to her expensive lair, the raptor flown home with fresh meat.

"Popular, this buddy of yours."

"Not at all. And that's relevant information."

Next, hugging four Whole Foods bags and a corpulent angora cat, Alonzo came lumbering along. A scratch on the back of his right hand was leaching blood. The cat yawned lavishly, parting its pink mouth to bare very white fangs. Then it nipped two vicious times at Alonzo's thumb.

"She'll bite me if I put her down, she'll bite me if I keep holding her. Damned if you do and damned if you don't. Mrs. Merrithew, she doesn't want cat hair on her new organza blouse. Or on her new cat purse. So I get stuck carrying Anastasia. But Anastasia, she's in a really bad mood because she just came from the vet's and got a pedicure. That always makes her really mad. Almost as mad as Mrs. Merrithew." It suddenly dawned on him that we were strangers and he swiftly channeled his employer. "Who do you want to see? Are you delivering something?"

"We're friends of Jon Kim."

"Jon Kim—the *maricon*. I don't know the Korean word for that."

"It's *kimchi*," Roberto told him in English, "it means 'hot stuff.'" Then he and Alonzo conducted an extended exchange in Spanish. Roberto kept nodding, sympathizing, I assumed, about being employed by such a diva. Then Anastasia again punctured Alonzo's hand.

"Jon Kim moved out," Alonzo said in English. "Quite a while ago. He came back from a conference in Singapore, and his wife had all the locks changed, so they had a big fight. Right here in the lobby. The superintendent told me all about it. He yelled at her, he threatened her life. He said, 'I can break your neck like a chicken bone. Any time I choose. I'm a black belt and blah-blah-blah.' The superintendent threw him out of the building. See that boxwood? *Stop it, Anastasia.* Where the hedge is all caved in? *Little bitch!* That's where he landed when he fell. Jon Kim, the *maricon*. He was crying like a baby."

Roberto asked a few more questions in Spanish and Alonzo replied, then said, "I've got to get going and show Mrs. Merrithew my hand. She pays me extra when this stupid cat bites me. She's scared shitless I'll sue. That extra cash makes this dumb job worthwhile. And she gives me her old clothes, for my wife. Like this cashmere sweater Anastasia scratched, and this negligee Mrs. Merrithew stained with her Bloody Mary. My wife's very clever, she can fix anything. But Jon Kim's wife, now she's really smart. She's an M.B.A. from Harvard."

Fluffy cat in bleeding hand, Alonzo watched to be sure we both left the premises. Roberto paraphrased the information he'd gleaned. "Guess where Jon Kim met Rudy Schmitz? According to the super, anyway. In the bird sanctuary across Memorial Drive."

"A notorious cruising area."

"He'd been warned by the police. I mean, a guy in a three-piece suit and wingtips isn't a very convincing birdwatcher. Especially with his pants down in a field of cat-o-nine-tails. And the rumor mill in the condominium says this Kim's personality had changed. He'd become crazier, more confrontational."

We were walking toward the trolley stop outside Mount Auburn Hospital, where a group of young people in scrubs were clustering.

"A restraining order. What does it take to get one of those?"

"Threatening someone. Threatening to break your wife's neck would do the trick. And brawling with your super would help."

"Genevieve Courson died from a neck injury. As the result of someone using his hands. Of course, the police would know about the restraining order. And all of us were questioned, all of the trustees. The night I found Genevieve, the night of the trustees' meeting."

The trolley crept toward us, making that pinging, outer-space sound in the wires overhead.

"But why would Jon kill Genevieve Courson? He wouldn't have been involved with her while playing in the bulrushes and coming out."

"But if his marriage was crumbling and he'd dated Genevieve as an alternative to Emily or as a beard… Then realized he was gay and tried to dump her, but perhaps she wasn't willing to go easily. Perhaps she had a few requests, a few *demands*… And if she had a bun in the oven that could give his wife more ammo for their divorce…"

It was becoming evident that Jon Kim was a suspect *in something*.

Chapter Twenty-five

The woman in the Shawmut College registrar's office, Trudie, gave me Fletcher Coombs' new address, a condominium in a former warehouse in South Boston, in the area between the new Moakely Courthouse and Fan Pier. It was a hulking building made of granite the color of a dirty snow pile, snow soaking up exhaust in a shopping center parking lot for weeks. It dominated its own pier in the choppy, cloudy water of Boston Harbor.

In the North End, such structures had been transformed into costly quarters for people and corporations. Through the massive plate glass doors, I could peer past the lobby down a long, dim corridor littered with drop cloths, a ladder, and rolls of what could be carpeting or insulation. Plainly, this place was under construction, and Fletcher was living in one of the first completed units. Fletcher buzzed me in without waiting for me to identify myself, so I assumed the developer must have trained hidden security cameras onto the entrance.

In the lobby, a fake birch kept company with a marble waterfall adhering to one wall; its cascade had been turned off for some time. The basin had collected its share of trash—a coffee cup, some plastic straws, a losing scratch ticket. An elevator, padded in the manner of a lunatic's cell, transported me silently to the top floor, where, in the distance, Fletcher waved in the light flooding over his threshold. "Mark."

"What a great place."

His Superbowl T-shirt was speckled with paint, as were his putty-gray shorts, and the expensive sneakers he'd sported the first time I'd seen him. "What's up?"

"Your view is spectacular." Which it was. So much had happened since I'd spoken with him last that I was unsure how much I should divulge. Should I mention Jon Kim and his possible interest in Genevieve, his alleged temper and propensity to violence?

"Larry Courson told me you've spoken to him."

That sure preempted me.

"Twice. At Mingo House and in the Public Garden."

"He contacted me, I didn't contact him."

"Same here. He phoned… So, you're upset about my film career, so Larry says. At least you're not like that horny Asian guy. The big software honcho. He kept hitting on me again and again. He even offered to pay me. 'I'll pay you in blow,' he said. 'A blow for a blow.' He thought that was hilarious."

So Jon Kim was capable of propositioning a young male beyond an anonymous cruising site. What about a young female? The condo was sparsely furnished, with just three blue beanbag chairs facing a runt of a television, and a portable bar stocked mostly with tequila. No posters adorned the gesso-white walls, of Renoir ladies or anything else.

"It was just for money, just a business transaction—the movies… Hey, Larry thinks Jon Kim killed Genevieve. I can believe that. These executive types, they're used to getting their own way. They say, 'Jump,' you say, 'How high?' 'My way or the highway,' that mind-set."

Fletcher went to the kitchen and got us each a glass of the pomegranate-strawberry beverage.

"Jon Kim knows judo or something. I know because he used it on me, in the men's room at Flex. I was taking a leak and just as I'm finishing, ready to zip up, he gets me in a headlock and starts kissing me. Which, no offense, I found gross as hell. I mean, Genevieve was right outside the door. Eating raw eel with Rudy Shits and his cronies. That Kim is a strong bastard. I thought he was going to *strangle* me."

So he did have a temper, he was sexually aggressive, the Korean Wonder Boy, as Sam Ahearn called him. And this was first-hand testimony, so to speak.

"But who was the father of Genevieve's baby? Whoever was the father probably didn't kill her. If he knew she was pregnant."

"Genevieve didn't have many morals. I hate to say it, but it's true."

"Bryce Rossi believed he was the child's father." I was curious to see whether Fletcher would disparage Bryce Rossi's masculinity, the way so many others so readily had—or whether he saw beyond the fey exterior to discern the fence and heterosexual.

"Bryce lectured at Shawmut. He gave a talk about Biblical archaeology, King Herod's palaces. How Herod was a great builder. He didn't just kill all those babies."

"Bryce had done time. He'd fenced stolen art. He supposedly thought there was a robbery in the works. Targeting Mingo House, maybe stealing the monstrance of King Charles the First… Did you know Genevieve was a Mingo? Through her mother?"

"Well, I knew she thought she was. But she had so many big ideas. She thought she could do anything. Get away with anything. And look what happened. It's horrible."

Pounding commenced in the building, several floors below.

"This place is a work in progress," Fletcher said. "I'm kind of being the handyman. They let me live here on the cheap."

I needed the bathroom, used it, and glanced into the bedroom—at a sight that transfixed me. In the middle of the floor sat a fantastic contraption, a bit of Jules Verne imagining the Internet. It was a computer, sheathed in a carved walnut cabinet, with red velvet armrests projecting from its sides and a brass tray enclosing the keyboard. Small brass heads, of Athena or Medusa, guarded the velvet-lined mousepad. Some thumbtacks needed hammering into the upholstery and the whole thing reeked of glue.

Scattered throughout the bedroom were pieces from Victorian furniture—legs from chairs, handles from bureaus, finials, a bell, the pineapple posters of a dismembered bed, and architectural items—a pediment of gilded plaster, a frieze of mermaids from some bank or burial vault, and all sorts of doorknobs, of brass and porcelain, of clear and amethyst glass. It was a Victorian body shop, complete with jars of nails, cans of varnish, files, a chisel, *hammers*. I hadn't yet heard the term "steampunk" back then, the movement to graft technology with the antique.

Fletcher had come up behind me. "It's my hobby. I like making things. It relaxes me after studying all day. I think technology is making us all less human. I'm very keen on craftsmanship. So many things made today are just slapped together. I hate that. Someday, I'd like to live in an Arts and Crafts house. Nothing lavish, just something made with care."

"So this terminal—"

"It's just a regular Apple. But I've customized it. Covered up the plastic, given it some character."

On the bed, a bland thing minus even a headboard, he had sorted out parts taken from period jewelry—pallid rubies, peridot, some moonstones and jet, and cheap clasps from bracelets and watch fobs.

"Is that gold?"

"No, it's pinchbeck."

I had heard the term somewhere. "What's that?"

"It's an alloy made from copper and zinc. It was used in cheaper—less expensive—jewelry. I use that stuff for ornamentation. You know, finishing touches."

His other projects included a microwave oven on wrought-iron legs and a Bose radio in the belly of a gilded griffin. He had yet to fuse any antique tidbits onto his Patriots memorabilia.

"Did Genevieve help you in any of this?"

"She thought it was stupid."

To his chagrin. "I felt I had to see you. Just to talk. After Larry Courson saw me. I figured you were his friend too."

"The guy's been through so much."

"Did you tell the police about Larry calling you?"

"Of course not."

"I figured he'd be long gone by the time they got to Mingo House or the Public Garden. It's so easy to disappear in the city."

Yes, Fletcher was obsessed with the past—as in thrall to it as Genevieve or Bryce Rossi. Did he want to live its ideals, revive its restrictions? Beyond the whims of attendees at Dickens fairs or the men who reenact the Battle of Gettysburg? Had he killed for that ideal? Used a dead girl for his own private *tableau vivant*?

Walking back through Quincy Market, I heard a gaggle of drinkers at one of the pseudo-colonial bars excitedly mention the "Victorian Girl." Wasn't it "amazing" that the case should break open so suddenly? So I elbowed through the crowd, past the wooden dummy of John Hancock hoisting a stein of beer and the resin lobster in a powdered wig, to watch Marcia Haight on a widescreen TV, summing up the day's events. Larry Courson had been arrested in a motel in Pawtucket, Rhode Island, in the company of a twelve-year-old Providence girl, Laura Petacci, who had been missing from a camp at Indian Lake since morning. So he was a liar, a pedophile, who used his dead daughter as a ghoulish prop in his act for sympathy. He had no empathy, no compassion, for the young girls whose lives he had defiled for his own pleasure.

"And, to repeat, there's also been a break in the actual murder of Courson's own daughter, Genevieve, the so-called Victorian Girl, whose slaying captivated the entire world. A software executive with ties to Mingo House, the historic site and scene of the crime, has been picked up by police and taken in for questioning. His name has not yet been released…"

The only software executive with ties to Mingo House was of course Jon Kim. Had Larry Courson tried to find him, tried to kill him, failed, and, upon capture, voiced his suspicions to the police, prompting Jon Kim to be interrogated? Wouldn't Larry's credibility be zero, considering his actions, especially being caught with an underage girl? But the restraining order would be seen as damning for Jon, as would his fight with the super at the condo.

Fletcher, independently, had pegged Jon Kim as violent. Who knows, maybe Rudy Schmitz had aided the authorities, monitoring his "Jonny" even while bedding him. That could be in character; this Mingo House crowd was so duplicitous…

"Can you believe it? It *is* the Korean," Roberto said when I arrived home. "One report says they found a silk cord with Genevieve's DNA on it at the suspect's apartment. And guess what? The suspect had thousands of Ativan stashed at his place in the South End. Rudy Schmitz must be mega-mortified. Not to mention newly single."

"But would Jon Kim play Victorian dress-up with Genevieve? He's all about technology and *now*. And would he kill his own child? If he thought her child was his?"

"Look at what Alonzo said. About his threats. Breaking his wife's neck—"

"But Emily Kim hasn't been murdered."

"He led a double life, sexually. He'd become a drug addict. People get hooked, they have pushers, they become desperate. You told me his company was in trouble. He'd shacked with that sleazy Rudy Schmitz. I know of at least four people who've called the attorney general's office, complaining about their contracts with Flex. About roaches in the locker room and broken treadmills..."

"What's Jon Kim's motive for killing Genevieve?"

"Blackmail, who knows? Maybe Genevieve took some embarrassing photographs. Needing money for school. And Kim, you know, over-reacted."

"Yeah, strangulation is a tad overreacting. And dressing her up?"

"She was already dressed up. She dressed herself up. No one could have fitted her and then killed her. It's too time-consuming. Chloe solved that."

"Jon Kim was due at Mingo House for a meeting of the board of trustees. If he were planning to murder Genevieve—or anyone else—he wouldn't plan it in a place where his friends and colleagues were due any minute!"

"Maybe it wasn't planned. Maybe it was spontaneous."

"I knew this guy. Well, I thought I did."

"*Thought* is the operative word," Roberto said. "You can't argue with DNA, Mark."

Chapter Twenty-six

Rudy now re-thought his relationship with Jon Kim. "He didn't really have background. His parents ran a hardware store. Jon would help customers find the right kind of screw. As a child. It seems somehow appropriate… And he actually permitted a drug dealer to enter my home. He told me that. Some former medical student who peddled tranquilizers. Imagine! Why that pusher could've stolen my Warhol. Or beaten us both senseless. But dope deranges people, doesn't it? So eventually he became entangled with that scrappy college girl, and ended up killing her. Tragic, tragic. Straight out of Aeschylus."

Rudy had distanced himself from Bryce Rossi too. "For all of his affectations, Bryce was basically a street tough. I mean, he knew art and wine and antiques, but he'd come from a hard-scrabble home. His father was a bookie and his mother was a nurse's aide. He'd served time in the big house: he had the most hideous tattoos that some pimp had applied to his arms. His cell mate, I suppose. It makes me shudder." Rudy believed Bryce was killed by "some thug" who'd materialized out of his past, to settle an old score. The police could make no sense of Bryce's tale that a burglary was imminent at Mingo House. "Perhaps it was his way to get us to pay for his services. Appraising everything. Who knows how these people's minds work?"

◇◇◇

Sam Ahearn had mixed feelings about the arrest. "Well, I was as shocked as anyone about the Korean Wonder Boy. He sure fooled me. I thought he was just a tense nerd in love with Rudy and his computer. Not necessarily in that order. But him going after a college kid like Genevieve, that's just incredible. I guess he got so he hated all women. What with his wife ditching him and then Genevieve wanting out."

The fundraising party, "An Evening with the Mingoes," would go on. Rudy Schmitz was adamant about that. It was needed more than ever after the "distractions" of the summer—the murders, the manhunt, the headlines spawned by the Victorian Girl. This was, in fact, an ideal time to refocus on the museum's core mission: to educate the public about Victorian domestic life. And the evening was an occasion to announce the founding of a new organization, The Mingo Circle, offering programs, lectures, and small teas to a paying membership. Seemingly, Bryce's murder and Jon Kim's arrest had made Rudy believe Mingo House might be "sustainable" after all.

And the party would be an exorcism, a cleansing of the karma of the earlier violence. "In a few years, the people who count will remember Mingo House for this party and its bright future," Rudy maintained. "Not for this period of…sordidness."

After the rain and humidity of the summer, "the deluge," as Roberto called it, the weather was finally improving. The sun reasserted itself, battling away the gloom and baking the sidewalks and rousing the flowerbeds in the Public Garden. The evening of the party was sultry, and suffused with golden sunlight, with shafts of sunlight pouring down from Maxfield Parrish clouds. The summer fragrance of new-mown lawns, perhaps from the Public Garden or the mall on Commonwealth Avenue, rode the warm wind and gave the evening the indolence of lazing in a pasture. Boston—the old houses of brick and brownstone, the London-ish chimney pots, the majestic trees—had never appeared more beautiful.

I'd bought a new suit and a red rose boutonniere for my buttonhole. I arrived at the premises early. Beacon Street thronged with the sort of laughing, chatting, air-kissing people you seldom see congregate in public. Roberto remained at home, ostensibly studying, but actually avoiding Rudy Schmitz, I was sure.

In Mingo House, the larger pieces of furniture had been shifted and cordoned off. Red velvet ropes also fended guests away from brittle knickknacks and chairs that beckoned but would collapse if used. The barren expanse of concrete and crabgrass out back had been weeded and renamed the "court-yard." It was beautified with rented palms, and its ailanthus trees strung with white fairy lights. Clara Mingo's gilded harp, restored through the generosity of Dorothea Jakes, was being plucked by a Taiwanese college student as guests filed into the high-ceilinged old rooms. For the first time in decades, Mingo House was hosting a party and everyone was enthralled.

"How enchanting!"

"You can almost imagine Louisa May Alcott…"

"And hear the clip-clop of a hansom cab…"

"I hope we don't offend the ghosts."

Rudy seemed elegant and somehow feline as he greeted guests, his face lighting up like the landmark Citgo sign in Kenmore Square whenever he spied a potential trustee. The VIP guests, who had shelled out a steeper fee, would be segregated in the courtyard to be cultivated by our current trustees.

Rudy addressed everyone in the library, making a speech about history and Mingo House that I found surprisingly heart-felt: "I greet you, one and all, as we begin a new chapter in the life of Mingo House, one of Boston's only historic houses, that preserves, intact, a slice of life from the turn-of a-century past. It is said that the past is prologue to the future, that we cannot know where we are going if we do not know where we have been. And how prescient that remark is, today, more than ever, in a world that is changing almost by the microsecond. Now, more than ever, we need the lessons of the past to inform and enrich our present."

The crowd in the hot, close library, which flowed out into Corinth One's bedroom, listened patiently.

"When I first came to Boston as a young student and entrepreneur—that was a while ago, before, in fact, the word entrepreneur had entered our everyday vocabulary—I was green and a bit bewildered, and I called home and related my feelings to my father. Now my dad was a no-nonsense fellow who ran our family store, Schmitz Brothers, in Baltimore. He was the son of an immigrant from a small village in the Black Forest who'd created a local institution out of dreams, grit, and perseverance. My father was not a sentimental man, but he knew the value of history, not just in terms of its physical remnants—houses, museums, antiques—but for what it can teach us all."

Dorothea Jakes, over by the shelf where we had discovered that morbid hair wreath, was speaking to a teenager in what seemed to be an angry tone, judging by her expression. The teenager turned, and I saw that it was her grandson, Chris.

"So when I told my dad that I just didn't get Boston, didn't relate to its intelligent but somewhat formal citizenry, he asked me, 'Have you studied New England's history? Have you read Van Wyck Brooks and Ralph Waldo Emerson and Bradford's account of Plymouth Plantation?' And here is where my involvement with this house originates. My dad said, 'Have you been to Mingo House? That in itself is a portal to the past.'"

Rudy went on, testifying how this historic property had "schooled" him in the culture and values of New England, thus making the case why the guests should become members of The Mingo Circle, become trustees, docents, volunteers, regular visitors. "We need you, the history of this city—irreplaceable, important, and endangered—needs you. Tonight, we are all Corinth and Clara's children. Well, I know that I am!"

Rudy won prolonged applause. And the puckered, flaking ceiling in the library was a ready and eloquent prop corroborating his pitch for donations.

I squeezed toward Dorothea, now alone.

"Well, we'll see if they break out their wallets," she said to me.

"Everyone really enjoyed the harp. Thanks again for restoring it." I couldn't resist adding, "The music is heavenly."

"Well, we've been dealing with a little hellion." She ate her fig hors d'oeuvre and nodded toward the young man now across the room, stuffing himself with mini crab-cakes. "My grandson, Chris, is on probation at Lenox. We hope he can stay. He's had a humdinger of a year."

Dorothea drank deep from her glass of fruit punch and elaborated. "Chris is quite the math prodigy. Two grades ahead of his peers. Unfortunately, he's equally ahead in…sowing his wild oats. He was caught in the girls' dormitory, showering with a girl at three AM. They couldn't sleep. Insomnia, they said. Then he failed English and just squeaked by in history. He'd been an honor student until his complexion went bad. It could be hormonal, I suppose."

"Aren't there prescriptions…?"

"Well, his parents are opposed to medicating children. My daughter-in-law read some book attacking Ritalin. And she thinks laser treatments cause cancer, so… She's adamant, stubborn, just like Chris."

Then Chris began descending the stairs, so Dorothea suggested we trail him. "I promised my son, his father, that I wouldn't let him out of my sight. His parents had a corporate commitment they couldn't skip, that's why he's with me."

Chris paused in the front hall, where he was staring at the placard in memory of Genevieve Courson. Balanced on an easel, it featured a full-color photograph of her shaking hands with Rudy. It cited her "extraordinary devotion to the Mingo House family." Genevieve herself had used that mawkish phrase on my first day of orientation. But for her that phrase bore literal truth, as I had just learned at Grace Torrance's in Rockport.

"Keep your eye on him, Mark," Dorothea said. "I have to pay the harpist."

Threading through the networking horde, I reached Chris, who had somehow procured a glass of punch. In the boy, I could discern the man forty years in the future, the country club alcoholic, all gin blossoms and right-wing indignation. "Incredible woman," he said, as much to the placard as to me.

"You knew her?"

"She worked here, dude." Around his wrist, he'd wound several bead-and-hemp friendship bracelets. He was bombed. "She gave our class a tour. Our whole class came here, see? She told us all about the ghosts and Mrs. Mingo being a psychic. She showed us awesome photographs of the Civil War. Heads in a bucket and this dude cut in half by a cannonball."

Genevieve had violated Mingo House policy by letting anyone see the horrifying record Clara Mingo had commissioned of Civil War carnage. Let alone a school group.

"She was a babe." He drained his punch and was eating the leftover lemon wedge, rind and all.

"Clara Mingo was a babe?"

"No, Genny, Genevieve Courson. She had a bod to die for." He had smeared mustard from the crab-cakes onto his rep tie with its design of lacrosse sticks.

"How would you know about Genevieve Courson's…body?" For me, that last word meant something devoid of sensuality.

"She came to my school. Later, as a speaker, through Shawmut College. She read from her paper about the Mingo family. How weird they all were and how they helped kill King George the Third."

"Charles the First."

"Whatever." He set his empty glass onto a Chinese teakwood table, and I moved it before it could spoil the inlaid marble top. "I was assigned to be her guide. To show her the campus after she gave her talk. We ended up walking out by the pond, and this tool shed was open. Hey, we balled like there was no tomorrow." Then his snickers morphed into sobs and he began wiping his tears onto his blazer sleeve.

Did I believe him? This pimply little preppie with a slight lisp? Oh, yes. *In vino, veritas.* And Genevieve Courson had led a freewheeling sex life, with men many years her senior. But she had to inherit *something* from her father. Why not a taste for young flesh?

"Dude, you look surprised. It wasn't my first time. I made it with a lifeguard in Edgartown last summer. This townie whose father owns a clam shack. But Genevieve was better. Way better. One of a kind."

I couldn't argue with that.

"But the life guard didn't get pregnant." He teetered a bit. "Genevieve did. She said it was no big deal. She'd had an abortion once before, when some Harvard guy knocked her up. I felt shitty when she got killed." He blew his nose and cleaned the mustard from his mouth with his handkerchief. "I felt shitty, but Gramma said it was a blessing, that Genny was just a goddamn tramp."

"Did Dorothea know *you* were the baby's father?"

He sighed. "Sort of." Chris almost knocked Genevieve's placard off its easel. I righted it.

"Gramma said the father could've been any number of people. How she once caught Genny kissing this German tourist. Right here. While his wife was in the bathroom. She said we'd keep it hush-hush. That was her word." He struggled to fix me with his bleary eyes. "Did you know her?"

"No." My answer surprised even me: "I don't really know anyone here."

What could I do with this information? Tell the police? I couldn't ask Dorothea Jakes; she was being groomed as a potential trustee, and could easily dismiss her grandson's boasting as "just the liquor talking." But she herself had disparaged his character, had portrayed him as indolent and sexually precocious, had made his claim seem plausible. Learning he was soon to become a father would rattle any high school sophomore. But if Chris had divulged the reason behind his behavior, he'd have sabotaged his future, compounded his problems, and no doubt gotten himself expelled. Chris certainly hadn't strangled Genevieve, and Dorothea, understandably, had protected her grandson, striven to keep him far from the garish spotlight, the seamy vortex surrounding the Victorian Girl.

I needed more punch. I ladled a glass, drank some, and ladled more. Miriam and Chloe were standing in the dining room, where the table laden with the pink and gilded Mingo china had been roped off and pushed flush with the wall.

Miriam seemed disturbed by the portrait of the Mingo triplets. "Victorian children always look so gloomy. It's like they're staring out at you through time, pleading to be rescued, even the privileged ones. You really wonder about their psychology. They seem squelched, somber, burdened."

"This is a posthumous portrait," I told her.

"How did they die?" asked a somber Chloe. The triplets were just about her age, but worlds away from BlackBerries, gummy worms, and crushes on skateboarders. Before I could reply, Chloe blurted, "Was *this* the room where the Victorian Girl was found? It *was*, wasn't it?"

Miriam confiscated the fig Chloe was handling but not eating. "I stipulated we wouldn't mention that, Chloe. That was a condition of your coming."

"The Mingo girls died of complications from diphtheria. And fever." Then, I swear the sad, contained expressions painted onto the little girls' faces seemed to grow even sadder, but that had to be the punch taking effect. The rocker where Genevieve had sat had been carted off for the evening, as had the mannequin, "Maude," too morbid to be present, and clashing with the placard commemorating the young docent, the dedicated student historian.

Sam Ahearn, overdressed in black tie, arrived, accompanied by a much younger Asian woman in a tangerine gown with a glittering rhinestone collar. "Well, I look like a goddamn fool, and I feel like one too. Rudy sent me an e-mail insisting trustees wear black tie."

"He rescinded that," I said. "In another e-mail."

Sam's wife, his second, I gathered, was a professor at Wellesley. She told us she taught French, which seemed strange until she explained that her family was from Saigon and she'd been raised in the Vietnamese colony in Paris. Madame Nhu was her godmother. "Such a lovely lady."

"Have you seen the help?" Sam asked. "Rudy's got some people in costume. College kids from the conservatories, if you please. Serving canapés down in the VIP section. Come, look."

So we all surveyed the scene from the dining room windows, and, sure enough, saw young women costumed as Victorian maids circulating among the high rollers, carrying caviar and lobster on silver trays from the Mingo family collection. It was very Merchant-Ivory.

"Isn't it…uncouth to have students in costume?" Sam said. "Given what happened to Genevieve Courson? In this very room?"

Chloe almost toppled a bisque dairymaid from her bamboo fretwork shelf. "Darling," Miriam said, "watch yourself. You almost smashed that."

"Rudy had them evacuate the Millet. It's being examined at the Museum of Fine Arts. Hey, look who's here. Wow, great to see you!" Sam said.

Nadia Gulbenkian's filmy red dress was cut low enough to display her weary décolletage and a necklace of knuckle-sized emeralds. Nadia was pursued by Henri.

"What magnificent stones," Miriam said.

Nadia ignored her. "There's a woman out front holding a cluster of balloons, if you can believe it. It looks like a Presidents' Day sale at a used car dealership. And she's wearing a Victorian dress. It doesn't have a bustle and it isn't green, but some tourists from Scotland took photographs. If the tabloids ever get wind of this, we're cooked. Cooked. Does Rudy have a brain? Mine might be addled, but it functions."

"Get a load of this, Nadia," Sam Ahearn said. "He's got college students out back. In costume, serving canapés."

"We never discussed this! Oh, horrors. It looks like a garden party during the Reagan administration. So much money and so little taste." Nadia broached the subject no one else dared touch. "I never cared for Jon Kim, but I'm glad he's okay. Given the circumstances."

"*What?*" several of us asked.

"I spoke with him. He's down in Hyannis. He's in trouble about his Ativan prescriptions, but the rest of the reports in the media were pure fiction. Hearsay from some blog or Weasel

News. He's not a suspect in…" Her eyes darted around the room. "They moved the chair, the one you found her in, Mark."

Chloe stepped back, as if to see how this revelation had changed my appearance.

"Chloe, you almost got that milkmaid. Again. Let's get you someplace safer, for all concerned." Miriam steered her away toward the front hall and its platters of brie, sushi, and mini crab-cakes.

"You're saying Jon Kim is absolved?" Sam tried to loosen his tie.

"It's a clip-on, honey. Remember? What you wanted," his wife said.

"It's strangling me," Sam complained.

"Mark," Nadia said. "Dorothea Jakes said Rudy is letting the MFA investigate the Millet." She appropriated my elbow. "Henri, you stay here and make sure no one busts up the china. And move that dairymaid. She keeps wobbling."

The front hall was ten degrees cooler, but its humidity was still bayou-thick. Outside, Chloe and Miriam were chatting with the balloon girl.

When she was certain no one else could hear her, Nadia whispered, "*Nosferatu.* Genevieve nicknamed a boy from Shawmut College Nosferatu. Because he drank something odd that turned his mouth red, like a vampire's. Your tongue is red from the punch, so it reminded me. That's what I'd wanted to tell you at the Soong Dynasty."

"Was the boyfriend Fletcher Coombs? Who drinks pomegranate juice?"

"Yes, exactly. That big kid with red hair. Quiet, kind of sullen. He came to the volunteer appreciation party Rudy threw at his house. Rudy found him quite fetching, as I recall."

That settled it. I said, "Fletcher Coombs did it. He killed Genevieve. Because Genevieve was free and easy with her favors, with every guy she met except him. And he'd known her forever and sort of felt he owned her. He's obsessed with the past. Not like Bryce or Rudy. He craves the ideas of the past, he craves its values. When women knew their place and couldn't vote or run. When women were weighted down by big, huge dresses with bustles."

"But for a college kid to kill his girlfriend... To have worked up all that hate during such a short life..."

"She had betrayed him by rebuffing his advances. And getting pregnant by an unsuitable man. By Bryce Rossi, Fletcher thought. The irony is, the real father of Genevieve's baby was Chris Jakes. Dorothea's fifteen-year-old grandson."

"*Chris?*" Nadia boomed, loud enough to wake the dead. "With the lisp and all that acne?"

"Please keep it down."

"Sorry. Oh, what a tragedy. What a sorry, sorry business."

"Chris told me himself, that he was the father. He's here. He's an alcoholic in training, he drinks like a fish. He says he met Genevieve when she gave the kids from Lenox a tour. Then Shawmut sent her to Lenox as a guest speaker. Chris got the job to show her their campus, and, well, they found a tool shed..."

"How appropriate. Dorothea claimed she'd caught Genevieve kissing the janitor in the broom closet. I thought she was exaggerating until I saw Genevieve rubbing tonsils with Bryce Rossi outside that awful Italian place on Newbury Street."

"May I take a bathroom break?" the balloon girl asked.

"Of course," Nadia said.

The president of Colony Bank sidled by, so we smiled.

"He's a rancid Republican," Nadia said. "...Well, if Coombs killed Bryce in a jealous rage, isn't Chris Jakes in danger?"

"Only if he blabs about Genevieve to Fletcher."

"Shouldn't you warn him? Or Dorothea?" Testing the brie, Nadia scowled. "I can warn him."

"No, I can do it. It's best if I go. Since he confided in me."

"Oh, here comes Henri. It's like being on a date with Interpol."

"Both of you are wanted," Henri said. "By Mr. Rudy Schmitz, in the courtyard. You and Mr. and Mrs. Sam Ahearn are supposed to mingle. By the way, the cheeses here are substandard. I hope the food is better out back. Under those hideous trees." As we traipsed downstairs, Henri grumbled that the Mingo House courtyard was an eyesore compared to the one at the Gardner Museum, lacking orchids, Roman amphora, or any aesthetic distinction whatsoever.

"Hey, we're lucky the potted palms are still alive," Sam Ahearn said. "They sprayed more chemicals on the weeds that were here than we used in the entire Vietnam War." Sam's wife blanched.

One of the Victorian maids, with a tattoo like bar code across her neck, requested we produce our credentials to be admitted, but Rudy swung by and snapped, "They're trustees for God's sake. Let then through." Then he assigned Nadia and Henri to butter up the Wentworths, and the Ahearns to charm an Indian-American biotech tycoon.

But, sometime, I had to slip away and tell my suspicions to the police. I could call, but showing up in person was more serious, more validating. First, I had to again find Dorothea Jakes.

The hors d'oeuvres here were delicious, briny, succulent lobster and the most tender scallops I'd ever encountered. Navigating the small space of the courtyard meant meeting the same shy fellow travelers again and again as their smiles faded, supplanted by intent stares at the fairy lights in the ailanthus trees or at an imaginary someone just beyond your right shoulder.

Then Rudy suggested I convince Gene Timmons, the owner of the South End's largest interior design firm, to become a trustee of Mingo House. Gene was a haughty man with a shaved head, halitosis, and a soul patch. He droned on and on in a critical monologue. "I realize the Mingoes were never top drawer, but I had no idea their taste was so pedestrian. This house could have been decorated by the late Tsarina Alexandra. She filled the palace at Tsarskoe Selo with furniture from Maples, in London. 'See Maples and die,' as the wags said back then. And Rudy Schmitz picked out the canapés, I can tell. His taste is equally dubious. Those crab-cakes are not *lump* crab-cakes, you can't fool me. Did you drive? I did, from Chestnut Hill. The valet in the parking lot is quite the stunner. I find you very attractive, in a certain light…"

He didn't consent to become a trustee. Neither did my other prospects, Nita Standish or Harry Bernstein, the owner of New England's most popular brand of canned clam chowder. I kept up my campaign to empty the punchbowl, just to make it through the evening; how I wished I had the company of my old friend Arthur Hilliard, Miriam's cousin, now happily living on Maui.

Then, by the bar, I again spied Dorothea Jakes. "Chris is three sheets to the wind. He reminds me of my father, I'm ashamed to say. And do you know why he's in his cups? Illegally, of course, he's fifteen. Because he keeps thinking about Genevieve Courson, that's why. He developed a schoolboy crush on her." She slapped a mosquito shopping along her arm. "More than a crush, really. She raped him. That's what they call it when a woman has sex with an underage male. She forced herself on him when she visited his school."

"Why was Genevieve at Lenox?"

"Shawmut sent her. She was rehearsing this piece—a theater piece about Meribel Boylston Sears. Don't bother looking her up, she's fictional. She was a character Genevieve created, from combining—well, stealing—anecdotes from unpublished diaries and correspondence. Of various Brahmin ladies of the late-nineteenth century."

Dorothea slurred the occasional word. Chris wasn't the only inebriate in the family.

"Genevieve got some of her knowledge of Victorian domestic life from interning here at Mingo House. And from cribbing from the Mingo family papers. Bills for brandy and paraffin and washboards and molasses. Corinth Two saved the mundane things, the impersonal things. And from Zack Meecham's work at Harvard. She knew you were a performer, she wanted to show you her script. She told me. She said, 'Mark Winslow can be useful. He used to do improv. He'll be sure to know good dialogue when he sees it.'"

"Did you see the script?"

"Oh, yes. A hundred times. I got more e-mails about that than from those Nigerians with millions of dollars they want to transfer—"

"Send it to me."

"I think it's a lot of bunk."

So her script was the "little something" I was slated to examine. I was yet another means to an end.

"Genevieve had the gall to tell Chris she was a Mingo herself. After she'd violated him amid the lawn mowers in that shed." Dorothea threw back her shoulders with indignation. "I've tired to feel compassion toward her, I've tried. I went to her funeral, as you know, and I even bought flowers to her shrine, you saw me. But I can't help thinking Jon Kim…did the world a favor."

Then a sheepish Chris came skulking up. "I feel better, Gramma." He'd neglected to buckle his belt. "I blew my dinner all over the bathroom."

Dorothea groaned.

"But I cleaned every bit of it up."

"Please promise me, *both of you*," I said. "Don't talk about Genevieve Courson at this party. *I mean it! That's crucial!*"

"That software guy killed her, right?" Chris said.

"Are you two driving home?"

"No, my son is picking us up right out front. Where the balloon girl was stationed. She's gone. She told Nadia Gulbenkian she'd only been paid for two hours' duty and she'd be damned if she'd stay one minute longer." Dorothea centered her grandson's tie. She frowned at his belt, which Chris finally buckled. "Chris, if you don't get your act together, you're liable to end up at someplace like Shawmut for college."

Rudy came beaming toward us. "Well, it's been a superb evening. If I say so myself. We have three new trustees. All with deep pockets. So the time is ripe for Nadia Gulbenkian to bid us adieu. And Sam Ahearn isn't really working out. Too negative and rough around the edges." He dropped his voice. "And the only person who mentioned our troubled software guru was Gene Timmons, the decorator, who said he was a dud in the sack."

"There are young people present, Rudy!" Dorothea said.

At that, Rudy retreated inside. Dorothea concluded it was time to go, so she phoned her son and I escorted the pair to the curb where Chris' father awaited, double-parked in a maroon Lexus.

So, at that point, I went sneaking away, straight toward the nearest police station. I ran through the warm, indigo night, the soles of my feet stinging as my wing-tips slapped the sidewalks and my boutonnière, hummingbird-quick, flew from my buttonhole.

I told the police everything—my own suspicions as confirmed by Nadia's new information. They listened in taut silence until one of them interrupted—"Have you seen Coombs *today*? We've looked for him, but he's not at Shawmut. And he's not in Lynn or Southie."

Of course I hadn't seen him since visiting his new apartment, with that room of dismembered Victorian furniture. The police thanked me, and made me promise to call them immediately if I saw Fletcher Coombs: "He could be dangerous." Fletcher's being a cop's son surely made this awkward, anguished for them.

Back at Mingo House, the hors d'oeuvres had withered and the guests were dwindling away. Rudy dismissed most of the faux-Victorian maids. He told Nadia she could leave, and the sushi chef from Flex, and the boy toy from Taipei who'd played the harp and seemingly usurped Jon Kim in his affections.

Rudy Schmitz had asked me to stay "until the last gun," and three students lingered, sweeping up, counting to be sure none of the Mingo family silver had emigrated, and picking up swizzle sticks, stray paper doilies, and, in the library, a fifty-dollar bill left orphaned on a hassock. "Well, the bill can't be Clara Mingo's since she was a contemporary of Ulysses S. Grant," Rudy laughed. "But she and Julia Dent Grant didn't see eye-to-eye. Julia thought Clara was a bit of a charlatan."

We were in the dining room—with the table laden with Clara Mingo's raspberry-pink and gilt china, isolated behind its red velvet rope, and the portrait of the forlorn triplets, seemingly mourning their own imminent demise. One of the college students spoke up: "Mr. Schmitz? This figurine got chipped." He indicated the bisque dairymaid that Miriam had worried Chloe might jeopardize. Henri had ignored Nadia's order to move her from her shaky fretwork shelf.

"Where?" Rudy sounded furious.

"See? On her bonnet. She's missing a bow."

"Well, did you see this happen? *Who* was responsible?"

"None of us saw it exactly. But we, um, caught Mr. and Mrs. Wentworth picking up the broken piece from the floor. They were feeling no pain, sir. They put away a whole bottle of Grey Goose between them. So the bartender said."

Rudy had told me Cal Wentworth had agreed to be a trustee. Suddenly subdued, he told the students, "You may go. Are all your colleagues done?"

"Everyone but valet parking."

"Fine. Thanks to all."

As the students herded down the front steps of Mingo House, one of them called back. "Here he is now."

My stomach went into freefall. "He" was Fletcher Coombs… decked out in high-Victorian fashion—in a black jacket trimmed with astrakhan wool along the lapels, and a vest embroidered with thistles in gold metallic thread.

"I didn't know you were signed on tonight," Rudy said.

"It was a last-minute change. I'm filling in for a friend," Fletcher said.

"Come in, come in, don't be bashful." Rudy, like the Wentworths, was feeling no pain. "Did you make much in tips?" Rudy slipped off his Hermès tie. "I had fun, but I'm still glad it's over."

Fletcher hesitated on the threshold, balking at entering Mingo House, entering the place where he had committed murder, one of his murders.

He seemed wary too of the placard on the easel, with the photograph of Genevieve Courson, *his* Genevieve. He unbuttoned his vest, sweltering on this night. "Things went well. We didn't get many complaints."

"Many? You shouldn't have had *any*." Rudy drew a long cigar from his jacket, and, defying museum regulations, ignited it with his Art Deco lighter. "So who gave you trouble? In the parking lot."

"That Timmons guy, the decorator. In the Escalade with the chrome lion hood ornament."

"Well, what happened? Speak up!"

Any move I made to call the police might trigger some sort of violence from Fletcher. I hoped we could keep things calm until he was paid, until he left.

Fletcher was blushing like a shy adolescent taking his first post-gym shower. "That Timmons tried to kiss me, but I fought him off."

Rudy exhaled cigar smoke and exasperation. "You *fought* Gene Timmons? Gene Timmons is a potential trustee. He's not some lout."

"He was hammered. He groped me. I gave him a good shove."

"You're kidding, I hope."

"No, I'm not."

"Oh, good heavens. Let me guess, you had an episode of homosexual panic." Rudy rested his cigar in one of Clara Mingo's sugar bowls. "Don't tell me you're shy. You certainly weren't shy in *Fresh Men Initiation*."

He's a murderer, I felt like telling Rudy. *Be careful, he's killed here before.* He killed Genevieve and then wrapped her in silk the way a spider stores its prey for later consumption.

"You weren't shy in that scene in the frat house. You went to town like there was no tomorrow."

"I'm not exactly proud of that." Now Fletcher stepped into the front hall, closing the heavy door behind him in a gesture I found ominous—not shutting the night out so much as shutting us in.

I had my hand on my cell phone but it was shaking.

"You can't assault one of my guests and expect to be paid." Rudy spoke the phrase in its now traditional manner, as all one word: "*Idon'tthinkso.*"

"You owe me. I worked, so you owe me." Fletcher shrugged off his period jacket.

As always, Rudy was oblivious as to how he was affecting another person. "Your sort just doesn't belong here. You just don't belong. I'm all for people pulling themselves up by their boot-straps, but some people will never belong." Now Rudy played the consummate martinet—the judge, the decider, the excluder. "If you shoved one of my guests, you weren't doing your job. I owe you nothing whatsover. You owe me an apology. Get out."

Fletcher draped his jacket over the red velvet rope. "You sound just like her," he said. He searched the dining room with his eyes, searched the space where the rosewood rocker had been. "You've moved things around. The rocker is gone. Where she was sitting—Genevieve."

The haughtiness in Rudy's expression dissolved.

"My God, it was you!" Rudy said. *"Good God, you killed her! It was you!"*

"She thought she belonged here. To the manor born. She thought she was Little Miss Mingo. 'I could stay here forever'— she said that."

Rudy pulled his cell phone from its holder on his hip. "You belong in prison."

Then Fletcher lunged toward Rudy, punching his face and knocking the cell phone from his hands.

"You little whore," Rudy gasped.

Fletcher kicked him in the groin and Rudy crashed against the dining room table, breaking bone china and sending silver-ware ringing to the floor. Fletcher wrestled Rudy past the velvet rope, into the newly restored harp—whose strings chimed, then snapped.

Fletcher seized Rudy by the shoulders and flung him—across the velvet rope and onto the dining room table, in a maelstrom of cutlery and china.

He would kill Rudy unless I could stop him, but what could be my weapon in this room where everything was fragile? No canes or walking sticks offered themselves, but, from the brass stand to the right of the fireplace, I pulled an iron poker—and swung it toward Fletcher until it hit his skull with a hideous crack.

He screamed, shuddered, and then fell to the floor, balling up like a dying cutworm as blood soaked through his hair onto the Mingoes' precious carpet...

Chapter Twenty-seven

But Fletcher Coombs was only wounded.

He was later convicted of first-degree murder in the deaths of Genevieve Courson and Bryce Rossi, and of manslaughter in the death of Rudy Schmitz, who'd suffered a stroke during the brawl at Mingo House. Fletcher was sentenced to spend the remainder of his "natural life" behind bars—and behind walls of cinderblock and coils of barbed wire, watched, regulated, and never alone, but perhaps, I thought, somewhat acculturated, having achieved the order he so craved at last.

His capture revived the media obsession with the Victorian Girl, as did the trial and imprisonment of Genevieve's father. Was it possible for a man as seasoned in deception, in seduction, as Larry Courson to arrange for the murder of his daughter's killer in prison? Time would tell.

By the evening of the party, the police were closing in on Fletcher Coombs. The media had gotten it wrong; Jon Kim was never a serious suspect. The police had lifted a fingerprint from one of the "Vengeance is mine" notes Fletcher had been depositing on the steps of Mingo House, matching it with a print Peggy O'Connell had provided on a term paper she had lent Fletcher for a class at Shawmut.

Fletcher's post-trial confession was broadcast live on CNN and all of the Boston channels. His jumpsuit was the orange of Halloween candy corn. Stubble darkened his neglected chin. He spoke with no more emotion that the narrator of choices on the average voice-mail menu.

"A promise is a promise. Genevieve promised herself to me. The month after we graduated from high school. We went to Nahant Beach, a bunch of us from St. Monica's. It was after hours, evening, when the police and the lifeguards had gone. We had a keg hidden, buried in the sand. Somebody had boiled lobsters and brought chicken and corn on the cob.

"There was this beautiful moon over Egg Rock. We drank and swam and played Frisbee. The water was so warm. There'd been a storm and it was full of kelp, full of seaweed. With big waves you could really ride. Some of the biggest I've ever seen."

Stress and despair had sculpted his physique. Was it possible, had his hairline receded?

"Eventually, most everyone drifted away so that it was just us—Genevieve and me, laughing and swimming and body-surfing. Then this big wave knocked me over and sort of tugged down my swim trunks, so I just took them off. She did the same thing. She looked so beautiful, more beautiful than I'd ever imagined. Without that makeup, without mascara. Just her.

"The east wind came up and she was shivering, so I kissed her, and she tasted of salt. I wanted to do more, right then and there in the water, but she said, 'No, I want to wait, I want it to be special. Because we're special, you're special. Just saying your name makes me smile.'

"'I'll wait for you,' I said. 'I'll wait for you. I'll be with you always.'"

Then he described that mild spring evening—that brought Genevieve Courson death and him ruin.

Fletcher had wanted to visit Mingo House, so he told Genevieve, to examine, close up, the joints of a mahogany side-board, and replicate them in a cabinet to enclose his television. He, in turn, would take Genevieve's photograph in a Victorian setting and in the Victorian-style gown she had sewn with the paid help of Cat Hodges and a pattern bought on the Internet. Genevieve would use the gown and photograph in her living history project, the monologue about the life of a young Brahmin woman.

She was trying the dress on, in Clara Mingo's dining room. Fletcher was kneeling, bent at her feet, ostensibly to inspect the carpentry of the sideboard. He was in modern dress, but his manners were as antique as Disraeli's. He presented Genevieve with a heart-shaped, velvet-lined box containing his hopes for the future as well as a 1/8-carat diamond set in genuine white gold, not pinchbeck. The metal was as pure, so he believed, as the love for her he had kindled since their childhood. Now he asked the woman he wanted to be his bride: "Will you marry me?"

"'You can't be serious!' Those were her exact words." She was carrying another man's child, she said. "'See? This dress is too tight.'" She had lunched with Bryce Rossi that noon at Villa D'Este. She was wearing the Eternity he had given her. He was writing her a check for $10,000, his first child support for their "little darling."

"It was the way she was smiling," Fletcher said. "It was a leer, it wasn't her. Her face, her voice—everything was wrong. She'd already killed the best parts of her.

"She said, 'I'm all set. Don't you see? This kid is my meal ticket. I've moved on. Don't you get it?'

"I asked her to kiss me. For old time's sake. So she came closer—so coy, so horrible. She pressed her finger against my lower lip. The way that con, Bryce Rossi, used to press my hand. Like it was all some joke. Me and everything else.

"I had a pair of white gloves, in my pocket, from my tool kit. The kind archivists and conservers use, to handle the furniture at Mingo House. I slipped them on. She didn't notice."

He coughed, blinked...

"I put my hands around her neck, gently at first... But she kept that awful leer on her face. So I squeezed and squeezed until the leer went away... Then I sat her in the rosewood rocker. She fit right in. That's what she wanted. She fit right in..."

◇◇◇

Jon Kim moved to San Jose, where he invented a successful video game, HistoryBlaster, based on combat with ghosts in a Victorian mansion. One of the ghosts, with gray hair bound in a ponytail, resembled a stylized Rudy Schmitz, except that it possessed the power to fly and breathe fire. Jon Kim had been cleared of any involvement in Genevieve Courson's murder but fined for his illegal drug use and ordered to perform community service in a halfway house.

None of the people Rudy Schmitz had cultivated on the evening of that disastrous fundraiser actually joined the Mingo House board of trustees; so, between them, Sam Ahearn and Nadia Gulbenkian recruited five of their friends and colleagues from the corporate, academic, and governmental worlds to expand and reinvigorate the board. With my help, they wrote a number of grant applications that resulted in Mingo House being awarded funding to replace its porous roof and bolster its fragile foundation.

During work on the fireplace in Corinth One's library, a mason discovered an ancient iron box secreted within the brick-work. The box contained a cache of English silver dating from the time of King Charles I—not a monstrance but an intricate salt cellar depicting St. George dispatching the dragon, as well as a chain, some coins, and a pick for removing earwax. So some guilty Mingo had concealed this treasure in the library, in the hearth—in the very spot Corinth Two alluded to in his "memoir." Indeed the silver was deemed to be stolen, being royal property missing since the time of Oliver Cromwell. Claimed by the Crown, it was presented, with apologies, by Sam Ahearn to the Duchess of Kent, in London.

Genevieve's script on the life of Meribel Bolyston Sears was published in the first issue of the new Mingo House newsletter, the memorial issue commemorating both Rudy Schmitz and Genevieve Courson, with their joint photograph from Genevieve's placard. (Sam Ahearn gave a copy to the Duchess of

Kent, so, for one brief, shining moment those two extinguished socialites glimmered through the consciousness of breathing British royalty, that is, if the Duchess ever bothered to thumb through it.)

To our surprise and consternation, the Museum of Fine Arts ruled the Mingo House "Millet" a clever fraud, done by a family of forgers. It was perpetrated by the Babineaux family of Rimouski, Quebec.

The house—"the curse" of Mingo House, as the media put it—reached out to harvest one more victim, a death utterly ignored because it happened years later. Christopher Jakes, an Amherst College junior, was killed climbing Mt. Leitzel in British Columbia when his grappling hook gave way and he plunged two-hundred terrifying feet to instantaneous death. "And he'd been sober for six months. There was no alcohol involved," his grandmother, long done with being a docent, told me. "Don't tell me that place, Mingo House, isn't cursed. Every atom of that building is evil."

I couldn't agree more. I resigned as a trustee two years after the murders. I have never set foot in Mingo House again.

To receive a free catalog of Poisoned Pen Press titles, please contact us in one of the following ways:

Phone: 1-800-421-3976
Facsimile: 1-480-949-1707
Email: info@poisonedpenpress.com
Website: www.poisonedpenpress.com

Poisoned Pen Press
6962 E. First Ave. Ste. 103
Scottsdale, AZ 85251